Camp Spirits

Abby Spector Ghost Mystery

Morgan Spellman

Meadow Cat Press

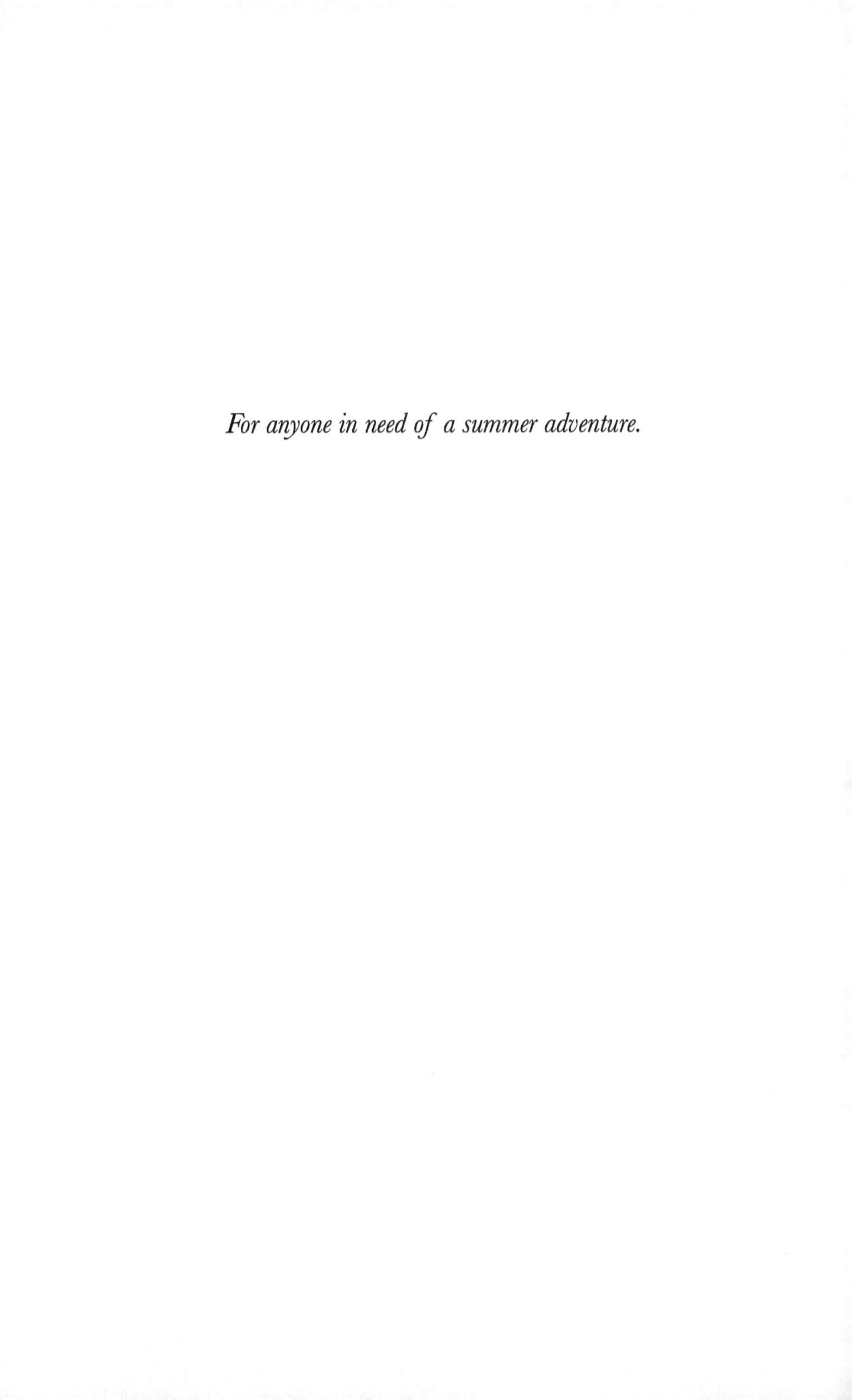

For anyone in need of a summer adventure.

Abby Spector Ghost Mystery Series

1. Say I Boo

2. Roses are Red, Violet is Dead

3. Camp Spirits

Camp Spirits

Chapter One

"I can't believe you talked me into this."

Sunlight spilled through the forest's canopy, cloaking Lucas in gold. Running a hand across his tightly coiled hair, he eyed a rather disintegrated piece of cloth, caked in dirt, beside his faded sneaker. "This could be evidence."

Abby turned to him in amusement. "Evidence of what? A late-night slumber party?"

"We're in the middle of the woods!" He gestured toward the curved dirt trail on either side of them. "Who knows how many dead bodies are buried back here."

"Will you relax? It's camp property. There haven't been any murders." Abby took a deep breath of hot summer air, wanting to savor the moment. In the few days since she'd started her new job at Camp Pine Whispers, her skin was quickly tanning and the sunburn she'd developed the first day had stopped itch-ing, so she'd call that a win. Since then, she'd covered herself in so much sunscreen and bug spray each morning, people could smell her coming. Noting an itch by her ankle, she reached into her crossbody bag to reapply the bug spray.

Lucas gave her a sidelong glance as he picked up the cloth and dropped it into the plastic trash bag he carried. "That we know of."

"Don't you think if someone had been murdered, we'd have seen their ghost?" Abby tapped the binoculars, which she wore on a strap around her neck, to emphasize her point, before coating herself in bug spray.

Lucas backed away, coughing. He choked out, "Next time, warn me before you do that."

"Sorry." Slipping the spray back into her pocket, she brushed the walkie-talkie resting on her hip, its bronze antenna glistening in the sun as it crackled faintly. Ever since she had learned these tools helped her communicate with ghosts, she brought them with her everywhere. Going out without them felt like leaving behind her phone—it made her jittery and anxious, worried she would miss an important encounter with a spirit. It was far better to get used to the soft hum of static that reassured her they were alone.

It was nice being out in the bright green woods filled with birdsong, with her best friend at her side. She just wished Mina could be here too. Mina would enjoy running the forest trails or doing yoga by the lake, with sand underfoot and mountains in the background. In the six months they'd been dating, she had never learned whether Mina preferred the mountains or the beach. She supposed it didn't matter—here, they had both.

Abby noticed Lucas watching her. "What?"

"You're quiet."

"Is that unusual?"

"For you, yes." Lucas shrugged, his gaze continuing to linger on her as if he was waiting for a certain response. When she remained quiet, he sighed and said, "I know you wanted to meet Sobbing Molly."

"I *want* to," Abby corrected, raising the binoculars as if that would cue Sobbing Molly's ghost to appear. It did nothing but confirm that they were alone. If there was any way to summon a spirit, Abby hadn't figured it out yet.

It had been four months since she had officially opened her paranormal investigation agency and she had only received a handful of paid cases—only one of which involved an actual ghost. She was tired of exploring so-called 'haunted' attics only to find squirrels, and explaining to grieving clients that no, she could not relay a message from their deceased grandmother because their grandmother's spirit was nowhere to be found. She needed to do something to get reviews up and new clients coming in.

So, when she saw an advertisement that Camp Pine Whispers was in need of summer counselors, she saw the perfect opportunity—revisit her childhood summer camp and capture footage of the infamous ghost to post on her website. Ghosts might not show up on camera, but their actions did. If they were lucky enough to get some footage of Sobbing Molly shaking some branches or stealing a pair of socks, all the better.

"We have all summer," Abby reminded him. She felt the words settle in her chest against another, deeper yearning— a yearning to hold on to time with Lucas as much as possible. Sure, this time, he was only moving to Massachusetts. And yes, Abby had her paranormal business, and a strong, supportive girlfriend who was very much alive and well. But Lucas had been a central part of her life for so long, and she had struggled so much when he'd gone to graduate school that she didn't like the thought of him leaving, even if it was only a few states away.

"Yes, well, once the campers arrive, I don't know how much time we'll have to run around looking for ghosts." Lucas wiped a bead of sweat from his brow with the back of his arm, careful to avoid touching his face with his gloves. "And she could just be a legend."

Abby scraped her sneakers through the dirt. He had a point. "But *everyone* talked about her. People *saw* her."

"Kids *claimed* to have seen her," Lucas countered. Relaxing his posture, he added gently, "Or maybe they really did see her. Maybe she only comes out once the campers get here."

Abby got the sense that he was only saying that to cheer her up. She flashed him an appreciative smile.

Lucas stretched, his athletic shirt bunching around his chest. She wasn't used to seeing him in athletic gear. While the ruby fabric contrasted with the cool tones of his dark brown skin, the sleeves were too bunched, the midsection too tight. He kept scratching or tugging on the collar like it irritated him. She suspected it was an old shirt that had spent the past few years neatly folded in the back of his dresser because Lucas refused to throw out something he might need one day. "Ghost or no ghost, I've got to admit, it wasn't a bad idea to spend the summer here. It's so peaceful and quiet. I drew a whole panel for my comic book last night."

"That's definitely going to change once the kids arrive."

A musky, unpleasant scent wafted over Abby as Lucas nudged the trash bag toward her. "If you're not going to pick up trash, the least you can do is hold it."

Wrinkling her nose, she wrapped her gloved hands around the bag. It was surprisingly heavy considering it contained mostly plastic. Abby nodded toward where the trail forked, one side heading back toward camp, the other blocked by a large, ominous sign: *Danger, Stay Out. Landslides.*

A footprint marred the dirt behind it. Someone clearly hadn't listened. "Do you think Sobbing Molly's treasure could be buried there?"

Lucas adjusted his glasses. "You know, I think the point of that story is that *she* was the treasure. Sure, her father was wealthy, but when his only child died, he lost his greatest treasure. So he abandoned his home and wandered the woods, never to be seen again."

Abby was all too familiar with the sting of grief. A knot formed in her stomach as she recalled Chelsea's mother sobbing into her shoulder, begging her to answer impossible questions—why her daughter had died, why the drunk driver hadn't seen her— and worst of all, the question Abby *could* answer, but hated: Why had Chelsea been out that night?

Abby pressed her hand against sun-kissed bark to ground her attention in the present conversation and not on the memory of Mrs. Summer's tear-filled eyes. "I prefer the version where treasure is actual treasure, like Black Beard's treasure. You know, piles of gold and jewels and what have you."

"Why would he have had pirate treasure?" Lucas asked skeptically, picking up a trampled candy wrapper and tossing it into the bag.

Abby took a quiet, shaky breath and said, "He could have been a pirate."

"He wasn't a pirate."

"How do you know?"

"If he was, they'd have mentioned that in the story."

Abby bit back a grin. This was the Lucas she missed. The one who would lightly banter with her for hours, making her feel like all the bugs and sunburn and harms of the world were far away, and they had nothing better to do than talk about made-up stories. "Maybe he was hiding out. Never told anyone. Would you tell people if you were a pirate with a bunch of stolen treasure buried in your backyard?"

Ahead, a twig snapped.

Abby glanced up. It sounded like it had come from above, where a gradual rocky incline leveled out to a wooded area off the path. She called out a friendly, "Hello!"

The breeze sighed through the trees, scattering shadows across the dirt trail. Abby reached out and touched the rocky incline. It was warm and surprisingly smooth against her palm, covered in small divots that would make for easy hand- and foot-holds. She half crawled, half climbed forward.

"Abby, wait!" Lucas called. "There could be landslides!"

Abby continued climbing. The odds that there would be one in the middle of a sunny day at this exact spot at this exact second were low. At least, she imagined they were. She didn't know much about odds, but she took risks all the time and had never gotten hurt. At least, not *seriously* hurt.

Someone was up there, and she wanted to know who. Sure, it could have been a wild animal, but that wouldn't explain the footprint. It was more likely a counselor who had wandered off the trail and needed to be steered back to camp. And yes, it was unlikely to be someone digging up secret buried treasure, but the possibility of it sent a thrill down her spine, hastening her climb.

At the top, Abby stood and brushed the dirt from her palms by rubbing them down her denim shorts. The rock she stood on fanned out until it met a grassy clearing, sprinkled with moss and wildflowers until it narrowed into a cluster of towering skinny trees.

Down below, Lucas was still shouting. "There could be snakes! Wasps! Bears! Bear traps!"

"Relax," Abby called back, starting toward the trees. "I'm not going far, just taking a quick look—"

"This place is restricted," a firm voice crackled through a walkie-talkie.

Abby spun around, expecting to see the summer camp director or a security guard, but there was nothing in the clearing except a beetle scurrying over an exposed root.

The faint electronic crackling grew louder.

Abby glanced at the walkie-talkie clipped to her jeans pocket. Hesitantly, she turned up the volume, her fingers brushing the brass antenna that allowed her to communicate with ghosts.

"Hello?"

A chill spread up Abby's right arm. If she hadn't known better, she might have thought a storm was blowing in, cooling the summer breeze. But she recognized the feeling of a ghost brushing her skin. She tensed with excitement. This could be her chance to speak to the legendary Sobbing Molly.

The walkie-talkie crackled as a stern, wispy voice replied through it. "This place is dangerous. You know better, Abby."

Abby froze, heart racing. This voice didn't sound like a child. And it knew her name. It couldn't be a ghost, right? She must have picked up some nearby frequency connected to the other counselors. But her hands trembled as she reached for the binoculars around her neck. This could be it. The moment she had been waiting for. The moment she found *her*.

The lopsided smile forever etched into her memory whirled through her thoughts—a kaleidoscope of bright red hair, warm green eyes, a face dotted with freckles. Dozens of memories flooded her—hands intertwined, lips brushing, her head in Chelsea's lap as nimble fingers stroked her hair.

Her breath hitched as she tightened her grip on the binoculars. As much as she wanted to reunite with Chelsea, fear rooted her to the spot. Fragments of dreams and nightmares bubbled to the surface— Chelsea's spirit, pale and deathly, contorting in anger as she shouted at Abby, blaming her for her death.

Despite her reservations, she steeled herself and peeked through the binoculars.

Chapter Two

Reality crept in as the sunlight dimmed and leaves turned gray through the binocular's lenses and the ghost of a teenage girl peered back at her. She seemed about the same size and age as Chelsea had been when she died, but the two looked nothing alike. Instead of Chelsea's wispy auburn locks, this ghost had thick dark hair braided in cornrows. Her intense brown eyes and deep bronze skin were far from Chelsea's pale freckled face and forest green eyes. Her muscles were toned, clad in a neatly pressed polo shirt adorned with the camp logo, khakis, and tennis shoes. Abby almost wondered if she was one of the other counselors until she noticed subtle differences. The girl's shirt was a different shade of green than the one Abby had been given when she arrived, the logo round instead of square.

Of course she wouldn't run into Chelsea's ghost here. Chelsea had never been to Camp Pine Whispers.

Her ghost wouldn't be roaming these woods, telling her to get out of restricted areas. And yet—for a moment, she had been so sure she would see her again. She let out a sigh, her emotions lapping her insides like waves —relief that this wasn't Chelsea coming back to haunt her, followed by disappointment that this wasn't the reunion she yearned for, and finally curiosity tinged with pity for this stranger who had died so young.

In the distance, a bell rang, its clear song muffled by the trees. The ghost glanced toward it, a wistful look softening her face.

This wasn't Sobbing Molly, the legendary child who had died long before the camp opened. This girl had been a counselor. And she knew Abby's name.

"Abby," Lucas called. "Time to head back."

Abby stepped closer to the ghost, who gestured toward camp, as if ushering Abby back. Abby tried to recall her childhood friends from summer camp, but none of them looked like the woman in front of her— and, more importantly, none of them were dead. "How do you know my name?"

The ghost blinked, looking Abby up and down. "I'm sorry, I thought you were someone else."

"You called me Abby," Abby said hesitantly.

"Yes, there was a camper, Abby Spector, who looks like you—are you related?"

"I'm Abby Spector," Abby admitted, wondering if the girl even knew she was a ghost. "I was a camper here once, a long time ago."

"It's me, Cassandra," the ghost said, as if that was supposed to mean something.

Abby racked her memory for any Cassandras she had known. At first, nothing came to her—other than her mother saying the name a few times. She focused on that thought until she remembered arguing with her mother about going back to camp. She had just started high school and her mother said she was too old for outdoor camp, and suggested she attend science camp instead. When Abby pushed back, her mother had shouted it wasn't safe, because *Cassandra* had gone missing. At the time, Abby hadn't thought much of it. Now she wished she'd paid more attention.

Abby gulped, wanting and dreading to know more. '*How did you die?*' sounded a bit too harsh, and she'd had bad experiences dropping the death news on spirits before, so she asked cautiously, "What are you doing out here?"

"Abby!" Lucas stormed up the rocky ledge, breathing heavily as he shook moss from his hair. "We've got to—"

He stopped short, eyes widening, as the walkie-talkie crackled his name. "Is that a ghost?"

Abby nodded.

"Sobbing Molly?" he asked, voice hitching.

"Cassandra."

Lucas looked thoughtful before arching an eyebrow. "The counselor who ran away?"

"I didn't run away." Cassandra's voice cut through the clearing. "I was murdered."

ABBY COULDN'T SHAKE Cassandra's declaration, but she met the other counselors in the parking lot and helped load trash bags on the back of a truck until her arms were sore and her T-shirt was stained with sweat. Lucas handed her a cooling towel, which she used to wipe her face. She draped it over the back of her neck and took a deep breath in relief. It kept her distracted as Carol Silverwood—the activity director and owner of Camp Pine Whispers—instructed them on team-building exercises and sorted them into groups.

Carol was a short, frizzy-haired woman who looked like she got along better with animals than people. But despite her grumpy expressions, she was surprisingly warm and welcoming in every interaction Abby had witnessed—currently, it was handing out harnesses.

Abby gave Carol a polite smile, took a harness, and stepped into it, tightening the straps. She scanned the trees for signs of an intruder, or any outsiders that could be passing by. The camp was isolated, miles from town. Sure, people camped out in the woods some-times, but not on camp property and *definitely* not in the area prone to landslides.

And Cassandra had died years ago. So, even if someone had killed her, they were far away by now.

"Concentrate, Abby," Lucas instructed as he took the cooling towel back from her and helped her onto a log balance beam a few feet off the ground.

She let out a heated sigh, wishing she had spent more time with Cassandra. After her shocking declara-tion of murder, she had disappeared, leaving no trace of her existence. Abby's foot slipped. She shot out her arms to steady herself, but it was too late. Wind rushed past her ears as she fell sideways.

Lucas's steady hands wrapped around her waist, helping her regain balance.

"Thanks."

"Concentrate," Lucas reminded her.

Abby focused on the log in front of her as she inched forward.

"Just a few more steps," another counselor encouraged. Abby didn't take her eyes off the log, but she could picture the elementary school teacher, with her enviable wavy blonde hair and cheerleader smile. She constantly spoke in an exaggeratedly high voice, like she was speaking to children. At first, this had annoyed Abby, but she quickly realized it was just an odd habit she must have picked up from being surrounded by kids all the time.

Abby took a few wobbly steps forward, keeping her arms out on either side of her.

"Do you do this often?" Abby grunted as she stumbled again. Three pairs of hands steadied her. She reached the end of the balance beam and jumped, landing in a pile of dry leaves.

"Once a year," the elementary school teacher replied. Abby got a look at the name tag plastered on her sleeveless polo, which read 'Sabrina' in bubbly pink letters beside a large doodle of a cat. "For ten years."

"You've been a counselor for ten years?" Considering Sabrina was the same height as Abby, with a youthful-looking face, she had thought she was barely out of high school. "And here I was worried Lucas and I would be the oldest ones here."

"Climb," Lucas instructed, giving Sabrina an apologetic look as he ushered Abby toward the climbing wall. He tapped the stopwatch looped around his neck, reminding Abby that it was a timed competition.

Since when did Lucas care about winning anything athletic? There wasn't even a prize involved. She supposed he was just trying to fit in with the more outdoorsy counselors. A decent effort was the least she could do, so she reached for the climbing wall, feeling for a sturdy grip.

"Not at all," said her third and final partner for this ridiculous exercise. With long, sun-bleached hair, tanned white skin, and a laid-back attitude, he gave off surfer vibes. The fact he wore a shark-tooth necklace only heightened the effect. His name tag consisted of a tree with the name 'Jason' in the corner. Seriously, had Abby missed the memo that they were supposed to draw pictures? She would have to add a rainbow flag to her own. "There's almost a dozen of us 'oldies,' as the kids call us."

Abby had climbed about two feet and was holding on to the wall, legs flailing as she tried to find proper footholds. She wasn't cut out for this. Mina, however, could probably scale this wall in seconds.

"They think anything over twenty-one is old," Sabrina said. "Right foot, ninety degrees to your left."

Abby moved in the direction Sabrina had specified, picturing Mina in one of her knotted T-shirts that revealed her strong brown arms. Like most of what Mina wore, her athletic clothes had small personalizations or embellishments—cut-off sleeves, cuffed sweatpants, or delicate patterns drawn with fabric paint. When Abby had first met Mina, her painted shoes had reminded her of Chelsea's bold creativity, and she expected to find Mina equally driven by artistic whims. But Mina's creativity was different—unlike Chelsea's ebbs and flows, Mina's artistic expression was steady, deeply grounded within her, appearing subtly but consistently. Abby hadn't seen Mina bubbling with excitement for a new art project or struggling with how to capture an emotion on paper, but when they talked late at night, it wasn't uncommon for Mina to have a needle in hand, sewing a decorative patch onto a dress or sweater that made it entirely her own.

She hoped Mina would find time to visit her soon. The last time they'd spoken—on Abby's drive to Camp Pine Whispers—Mina had reminded her she was about to start a new job. As a stunt performer, that wasn't unusual, but the first few days on a new set often called for long hours that left her drained and too tired to talk, much less visit.

Abby felt an ache forming between her shoulder blades as she pulled herself higher. She started to slip and dug tighter into the wall's plastic footholds.

"Careful," Sabrina called. "Just a few more inches and you'll be at the top!"

"I've got you if you fall," Lucas added. "You're only about eight feet off the ground."

Abby could tell he was trying to be reassuring, but

even eight feet would be a painful drop, if it weren't for the ropes. Thankfully, the ropes held her tight as she stretched until she felt the ridges of another sturdy grip.

"So you were both here that summer when a counselor went missing?" Abby kept her voice casual, trying not to make it too obvious as she peered over her shoulder to study their reactions.

Jason's eyebrows furrowed. "You mean Cass?"

Sabrina glanced down at her feet. "What a tragedy."

"You make it sound like she died," Jason countered, rolling his eyes as he reached for his metal water bottle. "She ran away."

Abby and Lucas exchanged glances. Even though Abby knew what the newspapers had said, it was strange hearing people talk about Cassandra as if she were still alive, when they'd just spoken to her ghost.

"Bummer no one's found her," Jason continued. "But she probably wants it that way. She's a fighter. I'm pretty sure she can take care of herself."

Abby was thankful they couldn't see her wince at his words. Cassandra might have been a fighter, but that didn't stop her from dying. She scrambled her way to the wooden platform at the top of the wall and caught her breath.

Her team cheered her on from down below. Sabrina's hair fanned around her shoulders, her pastel-pink nails glistening as she shielded her eyes from the sun. Jason stood tall, his slender frame casting a shadow over Lucas, who was trading furious glances between

Abby and his stopwatch. Across the obstacle course, their competition was seconds ahead.

"Lucas, you're next, buddy," Jason was saying as Abby climbed down a large net.

"I'd like to go last," Lucas protested.

"Newbies up first," Jason insisted.

As soon as she reached solid ground, Jason was unhooking her from her safety rope, attaching it to Lucas's harness. Lucas gave Abby a wide-eyed look that appeared to be a desperate plea for help. Abby pointed at his stopwatch. "You're the one who wanted to win this thing. Climb up there and win it."

Lucas tiptoed to the next part of the course—a rope net—with both hands clutching the rope supporting him.

Abby felt a hand on her back and jumped, before realizing it was Sabrina. "We don't like to talk about that summer," she said softly.

Not wanting to talk about a loss was something Abby could understand. After Chelsea's death, she went through phases—bouncing from wanting to be distracted and avoid all thoughts of Chelsea to needing to talk about her every second she was awake. Chelsea's friends and family all mourned her differently. "Were you close?"

A pained expression crossed Sabrina's face, but she shook her head as she tucked a strand of hair behind her ear. "I wish I'd known her better. Do you want help with your harness? One of us should help Jason spot Lucas."

Abby glanced to where Lucas clung to the rope

ladder with both fists, his feet planted firmly on the ground.

"It'll be a while before he gets the nerve to start climbing," Abby speculated, unclipping the belt around her waist. "But you can go, I've got this."

A group of counselors cheered, having completed the obstacle course. As their applause rang through the clearing, Abby wondered if they were the key to the truth about what happened to Cassandra.

Chapter Three

Dinner at Camp Pine Whispers was remarkably tasty, considering it was served at wooden picnic tables in a stone pavilion surrounded by tall pines. The counselors barely filled two tables, leaving the rest of the pavilion empty, with a good view of the surrounding mountains in their blue-tinted haze.

Abby helped herself from a steaming bowl of stew, while Lucas piled breadsticks on his plate. His presence was comforting, his good mood contagious as he basked in the aftermath of conquering his fear of heights. Abby tried to eat quickly, hoping she would have enough personal time before bed to call Mina and revisit the woods where she had seen Cassandra's ghost. Sunlight still brushed the dining hall, but it was weakening as the sun crawled between nearby mountains. She reckoned she had another hour or so before twilight settled in.

"I'd like to give a big welcome to our new recruits!"

Surfer-dude Jason stood on the bench, wobbling the picnic table. A few bowls of soup splattered as everyone gave him their attention. "Lucas, Abby, Trail Tots—"

He nodded toward the collective of eighteen-year-olds, who seemed to embrace the nickname with excitement.

"You're one of us now!" Jason raised his can of root beer as if he wanted everyone to drink along. The Trail Tots and Lucas did. The remaining counselors did not.

"And to my good old friends! Hannah, welcome back for your third year in a row!"

There were a few rounds of applause as Hannah Hickles, a petite brunette about Abby's age who was far more in shape than Abby, blushed and attempted to hide her face behind her water bottle.

"And, Elena, this is your…fourth year?"

"Fifth," Elena corrected, with no hint of emotion, as she cut her hamburger cleanly in half. With her smokey-eye makeup, dark nails, and braided black hair, she reminded Abby of Wednesday Addams. Come to think of it, Abby was pretty sure she hadn't seen her smile once, throughout their entire orientation. Her name tag was the simplest of them all: her name in plain black ink.

"And then, of course, we have Nick and Sabrina, returning for their eleventh and eighth year—"

The applause grew louder now, as everyone joined in. Nick and Sabrina sat side by side, grinning their gorgeous smiles, waving as if they were prom king and queen. Abby wouldn't have been surprised if they had been crowned at prom. They certainly had the looks and the attitude to win. Nick was a fitness and lifestyle coach, bronze and muscular with a well-trimmed beard and dark brown hair tucked under a baseball cap. Half the younger counselors were often staring after him and sighing dreamily. Sabrina was just as gorgeous, but had a softer, quieter warmth that attracted people to her. She seemed like the kind of person who gifted home-made cookies to her neighbors and listened empathetically to the most mundane stories.

"And you," Nick replied, reaching across the table to fist-bump Jason. "Congrats on sixteen years, man! You've set a record: most time spent on Pine Whispers campgrounds."

"Nah, that would go to Paxton," Jason said, slipping back into his seat on the bench.

Abby turned to Paxton, an approachable-looking brown-haired guy with a pale complexion and a few freckles. He couldn't have been more than a few years older than Abby, and while he was fit, his muscles weren't as pronounced as Nick's and he was significantly shorter. He didn't have the same 'the wilderness is my lifestyle, bro' vibe Jason had. He was wearing flip-flops and a high-tech watch, drinking a bottled Frappuccino.

"You've spent more than sixteen years here?" Abby asked, unable to contain her curiosity. He looked like he would be stressed to survive a few days in the woods, let alone years.

"My parents own this place," Paxton explained. "This is only my third year as a counselor, but I've helped out almost every summer. And I technically live on the property. So, yeah, I've spent a lot of time here."

That would explain why he seemed less excited to be here than everyone else. Abby wondered if he even wanted to be here or if his parents signed him up for it the way her mom made her 'volunteer' at the university she worked at whenever Abby struggled to pay rent. Either way, Paxton living here was thrilling. He would know the grounds better than anyone. The police may have even shared information about Cassandra's death with his family that they hadn't disclosed publicly. She asked cautiously, "Have you ever seen a ghost?"

"You mean Sobbing Molly?" Paxton shook his head, flipping the bottle cap between his fingers. "I've got some good stories for you, though. Wait until we get a campfire going."

Abby considered asking about Cassandra, but thought it would be best to bring that up without such a wide audience. Paxton might feel more comfortable talking that way, and might share more. Instead, the child in her couldn't help but ask, "Do you think her treasure is real?"

"That urban legend?" Nick scoffed. "If it was, someone would have found it by now. Likely this guy."

Paxton rolled his eyes as Nick clapped him on the back, but his smile grew. "You wouldn't believe how much dirt I dug up as a kid, looking for that."

"The real treasure at Camp Pine Whispers is friendship," Jason declared in his laid-back surfer-dude voice. He even slapped his hand over his heart.

Abby expected people to laugh or scoff at this, but

several counselors clapped in applause. Lucas was one of them.

The counselors broke out into the Camp Pine Whispers theme song, which Abby hadn't bothered to learn. She pretended to mouth the words until a young woman in an apron and hairnet brought out a tray of warm brownies, which caused the singing to die down as everyone dug in.

When Lucas retreated to the kitchen to make his nightly mug of tea, Abby glanced at the mountains. They seemed to go on for miles, a pale-gray blue like ocean waves frozen in time. Abby wondered what it was like for Paxton to grow up here, with so many forest paths to explore. He must have had an endless supply of friends every summer. When the air cooled and trees frosted over, with no one around for miles, it must have been lonely.

And to think, Cassandra's ghost had been here that whole time, drifting through snowy forests, all alone.

"Are you going to eat that?" Lucas asked, pointing to the remainder of Abby's brownie.

"Yes," Abby said, though her stomach was tightening in frustration. If Cassandra had been murdered at summer camp, the murderer was long gone by now. It was too late to save Cassandra, and it wasn't like they were going to find the murder weapon lying around. Unless it was buried somewhere—

"Are you sure?" Lucas asked, his fingers inching toward her tray.

She slid her tray further from his reach, knocking it against Sabrina's cup, which tipped over. Abby watched helplessly as the water spilled across the wooden table, soaking Sabrina's crinkled napkin, before cascading directly into her lap. With a startled yelp, Sabrina jumped up, her sleeveless navy polo shirt and white shorts darkening.

"I'm sorry," Abby sputtered apologetically as Lucas grabbed a napkin and passed it to Sabrina. "It was an accident."

"I should hope so," Sabrina said lightly, taking the napkin and dabbing the spots where the water still dripped. "I'd hate to think I'd done something to make you hate me already."

"Again, we're so sorry," Lucas said, even though it hadn't been his fault. "Do you need any help cleaning up? I've got stain remover in my backpack."

When Abby had packed for the summer, she hadn't followed the recommended summer camp supply list her mother had sent her. But if she had, she wouldn't have expected 'stain remover' to be on there. That was all Lucas.

"It's just water," Sabrina pointed out. "It'll dry. And I suppose it'll give me the perfect excuse to head in early."

"I know what you mean." Lucas rubbed the back of his neck. "All that walking has got me exhausted."

"You'll get used to it." Sabrina gave him a reassuring smile. "I actually want to get back to my book."

"Oh, what book?" Lucas perked up, straightening his spine.

"I forget the name—something about a beach? It's for my book club."

"You're in a book club?" Lucas's jaw dropped. He was clearly impressed, but Abby wondered if—to someone who didn't know him very well, like Sabrina —it would come off condescending. She gently elbowed him. He shut his mouth and smiled in such a big sheepish way, he looked like a schoolboy with a crush.

Abby stared at him. *Was* he crushing on Sabrina? That certainly would explain his overenthusiasm to help her clean up—and to show off at the ropes course. She shook her head, biting back a frown. It wasn't that Sabrina *wasn't* his type, but Sabrina was more like the type of girl he followed around with puppy eyes in high school and less like the type that actually worked out.

"We mostly read rom-coms," Sabrina was saying about her book club.

"I love rom-coms," Lucas declared.

Abby nodded to show he was sincere. Just because it was unlikely to work out didn't mean Abby wasn't going to root for them. "He loves all books."

"I love all well-written books," Lucas corrected. "Unless they are too violent, gory or written by Nazis."

"I doubt a rom-com would be too violent or gory," said Abby. "So as long as your book isn't written by a Nazi, he'll like it."

"I highly doubt it is." Sabrina tucked a strand of hair behind her ear, looking at Lucas with a hesitant smile. "If you want, you can borrow it when I'm finished."

Lucas grinned. "I'd like that."

"Okay." Sabrina slipped her hands into her damp pockets. "Well, I'll see you around, then."

"See you." Lucas made an awkward pair of finger guns and a clicking sound that made Abby cringe. She expected Sabrina to laugh or back slowly away, but she returned the gesture, biting her lower lip and—smiling?

"What was that?" Abby whispered as soon as she was out of earshot.

"I don't know." Lucas buried his face in his hands. "I don't know why I did that!"

"Because you like her," Abby pressed. "I get it: she's pretty, into books. She's a little more outdoorsy than I'd expect you to go for, but then again, she's one of the least outdoorsy people here. Besides us."

Lucas groaned. "She's way out of my league."

Abby shook her head. She had seen the way she smiled at him. Maybe ten years ago they'd have been in different social circles, but Lucas had come a long way from being the shy boy who went speechless or stammered anytime his crush walked into the room. "She is not—"

"Hey, roomie!" Nick called, abruptly ending their whispered conversation as he held out a hand for Lucas to fist-bump. "Looks like we're cabin buddies."

"Great." Lucas forced a grin. As Nick turned his back, Lucas flashed Abby an 'I-don't-know-about-this' look. He waited until Nick was out of earshot before whispering, "How much do you want to bet that guy is an early riser? Who did you get?"

"You just want it to be Sabrina," Abby teased. Lucas shrugged, unable to deny it. She slung her bag over her shoulder and headed toward the end of the table, where their lists of cabin assignments had been taped to the wall. She had forgotten they'd be moving out of their orientation cabins tonight. That meant less time to see Cassandra and call Mina—if any at all. The campers would be arriving tomorrow and who knew when she would be free next. She scanned the list— seven cabins, labeled one through seven, with one being closest to the woods and seven being furthest. Her pulse quickened.

She was in cabin six along with stoic and unnerving Elena Cortez.

Chapter Four

A loud rattling sound woke Abby.

She opened her eyes to the knotted wooden ceiling and the feeling of being rocked on a boat. No, not a boat. Turning to the side of her bunk, she saw a pair of hands clenching the guard rail, inches from her face, rattling her bed.

Abby bolted up, her heart racing. It was only Elena.

"You missed breakfast," Elena said casually, as if she hadn't nearly given Abby a heart attack. "Your boyfriend is worried about you."

Abby rubbed her eyes, letting her heart rate settle as she breathed in the scent of freshly washed sleeping bags and polished wood. She might have been too tired to be at her sharpest, but she was sharp enough to know that she didn't have a boyfriend. "Who?"

"The scaredy-cat comic book guy."

"Lucas? He's just a friend." Abby reached for her

phone to check the time. A black screen stared back at her. No wonder her alarm hadn't gone off. She had forgotten to charge it overnight.

"Well, he freaked when you didn't show up. Wanted to send out a search party. I told him you were sleeping. He's right outside, waiting for proof."

Abby stumbled down the ladder in her faded *Psych* T-shirt and plaid pajama shorts, grimacing as she planted her bare feet on the chilly wooden floor. Goosebumps prickled the back of her legs as she hurried to the window to wave at a frazzled Lucas. Lucas shook his head, relief and annoyance crossing his face. Satisfied, Abby turned back to Elena. "What time is it?"

"Almost eight."

"I didn't hear your alarm go off."

"I don't use one." Elena shrugged. "I wake up at 6 a.m. on the dot, every day."

"Okay…" Abby returned to her bunk, where she plugged in her phone, and pulled down her duffle bag, rummaging through it until she found a pair of fuzzy socks and a lightweight sweater. "Next time, wake me."

"The kids are arriving," Elena said in a bored tone. "I'll go greet them. You can help them get settled."

Abby muttered a vague response. She slipped on a pair of flip-flops and hurried down a dirt trail to the restrooms. She didn't have time to shower, so she cleaned what she could in the sink, changed into jean shorts and a rainbow T-shirt, and covered herself in bug spray. By the time she stepped out, clusters of families spotted the trail, carrying luggage, filling reusable water bottles, or snapping pictures with the mountain backdrop.

Elena was heading toward their cabin, carrying a large pink trunk that could only belong to the young girl walking beside her. The girl sniffled, clutching a big stuffed cat and a drooping *Power Rangers* backpack. Thin blonde hair stuck to her tear-stained face.

"Abby will take it from here," Elena said, as their paths met on the cabin doorstep. "Abby, this is—"

"Lilly," Abby said, recalling the girl whose birthday party she had performed at last December. She didn't usually remember her clients' names, but Lilly and her family had made an impression on her, as they lived next door to Chelsea's house. Or what had been Chelsea's house, when she had been alive.

Lilly blinked through her tear-filled green eyes before a subtle smile of recognition played across her face. She threw herself at Abby, startling her, and wrapped her arms around her waist in a hug.

"What's wrong?" Abby asked gently.

When Lilly's sobs grew louder, with no response, Elena mouthed, "Homesick."

Abby hugged the girl tighter. While she couldn't remember a time she was homesick, she had strong memories of distracting Lucas when he missed home. Reading him a story usually did the trick. She wondered if that would work on Lilly or if she had other interests.

"Are you going to do a magic show?" Lilly broke the hug to wipe her tears.

"Maybe later." Abby knelt beside Lilly, feeling her

pocket for anything she could use for a trick. She was out of coins, and a gum wrapper wouldn't suffice. "Do you want to pick out your bed first? Want one by a window?"

Lilly's nose scrunched and her lips pinched together. "Can I have one by you?"

"Sure." Abby gently directed her into the spacious wood cabin. "You want the bunk under mine, or you want the top bunk beside mine?"

Lilly twisted the straps of her backpack. "Top."

"Get up there," Abby encouraged, returning outside for her trunk. She attempted to lift it, but it was surprisingly heavy. Thankfully, it had wheels. Wheeling the trunk into the cabin, she found Lilly sitting hesitantly on the edge of her bunk bed, hands wrapped around the straps of her backpack.

"Take your shoes off," Abby prompted. "Jump up and down on the bed, test it out. Make sure it's comfortable."

Lilly looked at Abby curiously, a slow grin crossing her face. She let her backpack slip from her shoulders, unfastened her Velcro sneakers, and took a tiny hop.

"Higher than that," Abby urged. The girl was small enough she could jump a good three feet in the air without hitting the roof.

Lilly's jumps grew slowly in vigor, her grin growing wider.

"Very good," Abby said. She pointed at the stuffed bear sticking out of Lilly's backpack. "Why don't you tuck in your animals? I have to make a quick phone call and then I'll do a magic trick."

Giggling, Lilly jumped higher, making a thumbs-up sign.

Abby checked her phone and found it partially charged, with low signal. She moved around the cabin, until the signal jumped to two bars. That would have to do.

Huddled in the back corner, she called Mina.

Abby felt a twinge of disappointment as it went to voicemail. In recent months, Mina had been making more of an effort to fill her life with friends and activities that made her happy, and Abby respected that. But between her morning running clubs and weekend hikes, there was less room for Abby. Wanting to be respectful, Abby swallowed back her feelings as she left a quick cheery message: "Hey, it's me. Call me when you get this. Can't wait to catch up."

She hung up with a sigh and scratched her chin. Sunlight filtered through the windows, casting bright stripes across the worn wooden floor and empty bunks' heavily decorated frames. Abby wondered if she should carve her and Mina's initials into her bunk—if that would solidify them forever or doom them to one final summer together. Of all the couples immortalized in the wood, how many remained together? How many remained *alive*? After all, Cassandra had spent the night in one of these cabins. She could have easily carved something into an aged headboard.

Abby's phone lit up with an incoming text from Mina. Two simple words that made her stare in confusion:

Turn around.

Abby did as Mina instructed. Her heart fluttered with warmth and bewilderment as she saw Mina leaning casually in the doorway, one hand resting on the doorframe, the other tucked into the front pocket of her jean shorts. A fitted lavender blouse accentuated her athletic figure, the sleeves rolled to her elbows, revealing the smooth brown skin of her forearms and a slender silver bracelet. A playful grin flickered across her face, warm eyes twinkling.

Abby ran forward, throwing herself into a warm embrace as she basked in Mina's familiar scent and those comforting arms that she had longed for. The hug soon turned into a passionate kiss that made more than Abby's heart throb as Lilly shouted *"oooh"* from across the room.

Abby broke the kiss to tuck a strand of Mina's dark hair behind her ears as she savored seeing her in person after months apart—the camera didn't capture the depth in her eyes or quite how smooth her lips looked, shimmering with gloss. "What are you doing here?"

"You know how I've been talking about getting back into nursing?"

"You finished renewing your license?" Abby asked, a sense of pride blooming in her chest. Mina had studied hard, and Abby had learned a thing or two about cleaning and dressing hypothetical wounds while helping her.

When Mina nodded, Abby pulled her into another hug. "I knew you could do it! You're going to be such a great nurse! Did you want to celebrate? My break isn't until next weekend, but I'll see if I can get someone to switch with me so we can grab dinner."

"Actually—" Mina chewed her lower lip. "We can have dinner every night this summer, without you taking any time off."

As Abby stared at her in confusion, trying to make sense of her words, Mina explained, "You're looking at the new camp nurse."

Abby's heart warmed. "No way!"

Mina's grin spread, her earrings sparkling with tiny rainbows. "I wanted to tell you earlier, but I wasn't able to get in until late last night, and Lucas said you liked surprises."

"I do." Abby stepped toward Mina until she was so close, Mina's breath warmed her nose. "Only when they are good surprises. Which this definitely is."

Abby felt Mina's comforting hands on her back as she leaned into a kiss. Mina's soft lips brushed hers, tasting faintly of coffee and coconut ChapStick. When they broke apart, Abby was grinning so wide her cheeks ached.

Mina was *here*, spending the summer with her. She had taken a job to be close to her. And sure, it was a temporary job, but for six glorious weeks she would have her two favorite people at her side. Camp Pine Whispers was starting to feel more like home than her apartment ever had.

"So what's this favor you need from me?" Mina asked.

Abby lowered her voice to make sure Lilly didn't

hear. With each jump, the bed creaked and the girl's smile grew wider, her hands waving wildly at her sides. "It can wait. When you get a chance, I'd like you to look up some information about a girl who went missing from here about ten years ago."

Mina frowned. "Do I want to know what this is about?"

Abby chewed her lip. "Lucas and I might have run into her ghost."

Mina's eyes widened, her breath hitching. Light glinted off her rings as she tucked her hair behind her triple-pierced ear. "I'll ask around the office and see what I can find online."

"Thank you, that would be amazing!" Abby pulled her in for another hug as Elena reappeared in the doorway.

"Incoming," Elena said, setting another suitcase by the closest bunk to the door. A dark-haired girl followed her in, eyes glued to the screen of her phone. "I could use a hand with the luggage."

Mina leaned closer to Abby. For a moment, Abby thought she was going to kiss her cheek, but instead she whispered against her ear. "Be careful."

Abby gently touched the pink salt pendant around her neck—the one Mina had given her for protection against dangerous spirits.

Mina's hand slipped from Abby's, a soft smile tugging at her lips. She turned to help a new camper with her luggage, and Abby felt a pleasant sense of excitement. Camp was only beginning and already her two favorite people were here with her and she had discovered a ghost.

This was going to be the perfect summer.

Chapter Five

Abby had every intention of finding Mina again soon, but between herding the campers to orientation, lunch, and a field where she led a game of capture the flag, she struggled to find time for bathroom breaks, let alone time to visit her girlfriend.

The first free time she had was when the kids started getting ready for bed. She pretended she needed to shower, left Elena in charge, and headed toward the Lodge, where Mina was staying.

The campgrounds were quiet in the dwindling evening light. Fireflies darted between wildflowers, lighting the hills with pale green flashes. The air cooled in a strengthening breeze that rustled loudly through leaves and branches, carrying a refreshing foresty scent with the faintest notes of campfire smoke.

It reminded Abby of the summers she spent with her grandparents, when she and her cousin Sam would stay up late looking at the stars and whispering secrets or deep-seated dreams about their future. It was hard to believe that over a decade had passed since then. In her dreams, she had imagined she would be married and famous by now. A movie star, or a Broadway actor, married to a cute Hollywood writer or director, planning out how they would rescue dolphins or adopt kids. But she didn't care about fame, not really. She loved the theatrics of show business, and was just as happy putting on sock-puppet productions for campers as she was on stage—as long as she could make an audience smile and laugh, have people walk away feeling a little better than when they walked in, she was happy.

Abby turned on her flashlight, casting long shadows against the dirt path. She supposed helping ghosts move on left her with a similar satisfaction as to a performance well done. Sure, the ghosts rarely applauded, but they were grateful—usually. And, once she helped a spirit move on, it left their loved ones a bit lighter.

"Wait up, Abby!" Lucas's voice made Abby jump, binoculars bouncing against her chest. She whirled around, shining her flashlight directly on him.

He winced, shielding his eyes, and held up his own flashlight in surrender.

Abby lowered the light, her hand flying to her heart. "Don't scare me like that."

"Don't wander off in the middle of the night by yourself," Lucas countered, rocks crunching under his sneakers as he joined her.

"It's not the middle of the night. The sun hasn't even fully set."

"I can't believe you're going to talk to that ghost again—"

Abby braced for him to tell her how dangerous it was, a retort on the tip of her tongue.

"—without me."

Abby turned to him in surprise. "You wanted to come with me to look for Cassandra?"

Lucas gave her an incredulous look. "I wouldn't be here if I didn't."

Abby chewed her lip. She could tell him that she was headed to see Mina, but she didn't want to push him away. And she *did* want to try to talk to Cassandra again. She ran her thumb over the antenna of the walkie-talkie on her hip. "I thought you didn't like the whole ghost investigation thing."

Lucas's glasses gleamed in the rays of her flashlight. He stuck his hand into the pocket of his sweatpants. "It took a bit of warming up to. It's a big adjustment, learning ghosts are real, seeing them up close. And I'll admit, it's still unnerving, not knowing what exactly they're capable of. But I've always admired how much you enjoy helping people. I like helping you help people. And ghosts are just people, right? So this ghost investigation thing—helping them move on—it's good. I'm proud of you."

Abby's heart warmed with the praise. She tried to think of a teasing remark, but it wouldn't come to her. So instead she said softly, "Thanks."

"Come on," Lucas said, gesturing toward the forest. "We better get going before anyone realizes we're missing."

Abby cast a sidelong glance toward the Lodge. She felt her romantic plans falling apart as her curiosity drew her toward Cassandra. With a sigh, she turned away from the Lodge, following Lucas into the forest.

Moonlight spotted the earth, dancing as branches swayed overhead in a gentle breeze. The distant sounds of campers getting ready for bed faded until they were immersed in rustling leaves and the chatter of insects. A few minutes in, the trees grew so thick and the sky so dark, they needed their flashlights to guide them.

Not long after, a voice crackled through the walkie-talkie. "Hello?"

Abby turned up the volume as she raised the binoculars.

Cassandra's ghost loomed in front of her, looking exactly as they had left her, in her camp uniform with her braided hair, a knobby bush slicing harmlessly through her striped socks.

"You came back," she said with a note of approval.

"As soon as I could," Abby admitted.

"How long has it been?" Cassandra asked.

"A little over a day."

Cassandra's brow wrinkled in confusion. "I tried to follow you. But I can't make it into camp. I just sort of…fade, I guess. It feels like seconds ago, but it's dark now."

Behind Abby, Lucas cleared his throat, clearly wanting to be introduced.

"This is Lucas, my paranormal investigation partner." Abby couldn't help but beam with pride as she introduced him, even though her stomach knotted at the thought that this might be the last time she said those words. She didn't want this summer to end.

Cassandra drifted toward Lucas, studying him closely. She took in his lean build, tight coiled hair, and sharp jawline as Lucas tapped his foot, nervously, as if sensing he was being watched. Cassandra's lips parted with a pleased look of recognition and Abby could imagine her laying this image over one of the shy, gangly boy Lucas had been when he was a camper.

"Ah, yes." Cassandra's voice crackled through the walkie-talkie. "You're the kid with stage fright."

"I don't have stage fright," Lucas objected, adjusting his glasses. "I just hate improv. Give me lines that I can memorize in advance and I will amaze you."

"He really will," Abby agreed. "You should hear him sing along to the *Hamilton* soundtrack."

Lucas grinned. "Thank you."

"What's *Hamilton*?" Cassandra asked.

"Only the greatest musical of the decade," Lucas said, frowning. "It must have come out after you…"

"Were murdered?" Cassandra finished, a cold look in her eyes.

Lucas scraped his sneaker across the dirt trail, nodding sheepishly. "Yeah, that."

"Why do you think you were murdered?" Abby asked slowly.

"Because I was," Cassandra said, amber eyes staring intensely at Abby. She broke eye contact to drift back and forth across the trail, as if pacing. "I was out at night, following someone. And then… I felt a sharp pain on the back of my head. And the next thing I know, I'm like this."

"This is where it happened?" Lucas gulped, his flashlight darting from the rocky incline on the left, which gradually descended toward the moonlit lake on the right.

Cassandra glanced toward camp, then back toward Lucas with a shrug. "Somewhere around here. I can't remember exactly."

"What cabin were you in?" Abby asked.

The lake lapped gently against the shore as Cassandra looked thoughtful. "Cabin two."

"You didn't happen to carve your initials or anything there, did you?"

At the same time, Lucas asked, "Who were you following?"

"No." Cassandra shut her eyes. "That's vandalism. And I can't remember. Elena, I think."

"Elena Cortez?"

"Yes," Cassandra said with a wistful sound. Her eyes pinched shut, lips forming a thin line as she added, "It was storming. I saw her sneak out and I went to stop her and...someone killed me."

Abby sucked in a breath. "You think Elena killed you?"

"*No*," Cassandra said adamantly. Her eyes fluttered open, her forehead crinkled with thought—or anger. "Elena would never. But she might know who did."

"It's a start," Abby admitted, unwilling to write Elena off so easily. Whether she was guilty or not, she was probably the last person to see Cassandra alive.

And she didn't tell anyone. That made her suspicious. "Do you remember anything else about that night?"

Cassandra shook her head. "It comes to me in pieces. The storm. Elena. Darkness." She reached toward Lucas's flashlight. The light barely flickered around her hand, as if uncertain of what to do with a ghost. "You know, I can't feel warmth anymore. Or the cold. I just am. It's not unpleasant. But it's not living."

Abby longed to reach out and embrace her, comfort her, but she knew her fingers would slip through her as easily as they slipped through mist. She settled with a sharp nod of acknowledgment and promised, "We'll help you move on."

A thoughtful expression crossed Cassandra's youthful face. "Okay. But first, I want to know what happened to me. Why I died."

Abby thought of Chelsea's mother asking the very same question about her daughter's death—her grief pouring through her gut-wrenching sobs. Somewhere out there, people must have done the same for Cassandra. They deserved answers.

"It could have been an accident," Lucas said gently. "You could have slipped and hit your head."

Abby winced at the thought, but Lucas was right. It could have been a series of unfortunate circumstances —a tree falling or a landslide caused by the storm.

"And no one ever found my body?"

Abby exchanged glances with Lucas. As much as it frightened her to admit it, murder was a possibility.

An awkward shuffling of his feet told Abby he was thinking along the same lines.

"We'll help you," Abby said. "But, even if we figure out what happened, there might not be a good answer to '*why*'."

"There rarely is," Cassandra said coldly. "But I need to know."

Chapter Six

Abby studied Elena closely over the next few days. Aside from streaming the occasional crime podcast through her headphones when she was supposed to be watching the campers, she was a model counselor. She showed up on time, helped the girls tie their shoes and braid their hair. She even sang along with camp songs. If she knew what happened to Cassandra, she certainly didn't seem to be weighed down by guilt.

As the sky darkened and the air cooled to a refreshing breeze, campers gathered around crackling campfires and begged for spooky stories.

"Elena seems like the spooky type," Jason offered. "Want to kick us off with a good ghost story?"

"Ghosts aren't real," Elena said flatly.

Across the campfire, Lucas raised an eyebrow as if to say 'are you sure about that?' Abby suppressed a laugh. She had missed their easy-going communication—the ability to have conversations without words. She hoped it wouldn't go away when he started his new job.

"Don't ruin their fun," Nick chimed in. As the air cooled, he had put on a sleeveless zip-up hoodie and left it unzipped, revealing his toned bronze arms. Abby didn't see how that was at all helpful against the evening breeze. "Why don't you tell the legend of Sobbing Molly?"

Several of the kids responded with awws or cheers, while others continued their whispered conversations as they snacked on s'mores.

Elena's eyes darkened and she snapped, "I said no, Nick!"

Her words cut through the evening air, loud against the crackling fire. The other campers fell silent, all eyes turning to Elena.

Paxton shifted his weight beside her and raised his hand. "Who wants to hear a ghost story?"

A bunch of jumbled responses followed, consisting mostly of 'me' and 'I do' and the occasional 'only if it's not too scary.'

"Alright, gather round." Paxton ran a hand through his messy hair as the last few campers settled cross-legged on the grass. "Over a hundred years ago— when these woods were thick and empty, home to only deer and bears and the like—a wealthy man passed through a nearby mining town and his wife fell in love with the mountains."

His voice slowed and deepened, sucking the campers in. Even Abby, who had heard this tale dozens of times, was drawn in. He'd make a good podcast host.

"Her husband loved her very much, so he was determined to find the perfect home for her here. He spent years surveying the land until he picked out the ideal spot, with the most gorgeous view, and he spent even more years building the perfect home. By the time they moved in, their daughter was nearly six, and his wife came down with the flu. The home was so remote, no doctors could make it up the mountains in the snow, and so the woman died."

For the first time, Abby felt a pang of sympathy at this part of the story. Mina had shared such loving memories about her mother, and how hard it was when she had lost her. She had given up nursing for years to avoid the pain of watching other families go through the same thing. It was funny how this story had once seemed so fun and exciting, but now seemed sad and tragic. It must have been the way Paxton told it.

Abby wasn't the only one who found this emotional. Hannah shifted closer to Jason, her eyes downcast. She shivered and Jason draped his arm over her shoulder. There was nothing overtly romantic about the gesture, but Abby found herself longing for the comfort of Mina's warm embrace. It wasn't lost on her that Mina had given up practically her entire summer to come here, to spend time with Abby. And—so far—Abby had spent hardly any of her free time visiting Mina. She should do something nice for her, like make her a flower crown, or weave her a basket. Who was she kidding—her baskets were less of a romantic gift and more of a gag gift—she would give one to her mom. At least the holes in the bottom could be useful as a flower planter.

"Despite his gorgeous new home, the man considered returning to the city," Paxton continued. "But his daughter loved the land so much, he decided to stay 'just one more year.' His daughter, Molly, loved to play in the woods. She said she had made friends with fairies and discovered secret worlds in the trees."

"Like Alice in Wonderland?" Lilly asked.

"Yes," said Paxton, pointing at Lilly as if to say 'that girl knows her stuff.' "Like Alice. Every year, her father would propose going back to the city and Molly would beg to stay 'just one more year' and her father would agree. This happened until Molly turned twelve, and their relatives came to visit. Her aunt was so appalled by Molly's bare feet and improper clothes that she insisted she bring Molly back to the city with her, so she could make friends her own age and learn to be more ladylike."

"You mean to get married," Elena chimed in.

Paxton gave her a disappointed look and shook his head, but he said, "And eventually to get married. Her father reluctantly agreed and, upon hearing this decision, Molly ran off into the woods and never returned."

Several of the girls shivered, looking over their shoulders as if they expected to see her wandering the dark. Jason smiled at Hannah and pulled her closer. She blushed, rolling her eyes, but made no move to pull away. Maybe that side hug had been romantic after all.

"Her father called a search party." Paxton's voice

rang over the crackling of the campfire and the rustling leaves. "They searched the woods for three days straight, but there was no sign of Molly."

Elena's face took on a dark, somber expression as she stared at the fire. Abby wondered if she was thinking of Cassandra and the aftermath of her disappearance. Did she know she was dead? Or did she merely think she had been missing for all these years?

"Her father spent the rest of the year in mourning, always leaving a light on in case she needed to find her way home. But once the winter passed and Molly had not returned, he left his home in the middle of the night and was never seen again. No one knows where he went, or if he found his daughter, but the legends say he buried his treasure and hid his home to keep his sister from getting a single cent—not after she had led to Molly's disappearance. And so, in an abandoned part of these very woods, they say his treasure still lies buried, waiting for someone to find it. And, if you listen carefully, you may be able to hear the ghost of poor lost Molly, sobbing in the woods, or her father calling for her."

A tense silence followed, in which the fire crackled loudly, sending tendrils of smoke into the starlit sky.

A girl let out a faint sob and began to cry.

Sabrina put a reassuring hand on the crying girl's back. "It's just a story. There's nothing in these woods except trees and critters."

"Who wants another s'more?" Jason offered, reaching for a box of graham crackers. He raddled it toward the crying girl.

Tons of kids got up, scrambling toward him with enthusiastic shouts. A few of them began chanting for s'mores.

Hannah slipped the box from his fingers, her pale hands flickering in the firelight. "Alright, anyone who wants s'mores, line up here—"

As a line began to form, Elena stood without a word and retreated into the cabin, letting the door slam shut behind her.

ELENA WOULDN'T SPEAK to Abby—not unless it was about the next activity. Even though she slept a few feet away, her bunk woven with blue fairy lights, Abby felt like there was a mountain between them. The afternoon bell rang and campers scrambled from picnic tables, leaving half-finished paper fans and scribbled drawings. Three campers remained, at various tables, meticulously finishing their art pieces. Abby moved to an empty table and packed up a box of art supplies, scanning her surroundings for Elena.

Located on a hill, the art pavilion's open walls gave her a 360-vantage point of the campgrounds. She supposed it was so painters could take in the magnificent view of the glimmering lake, with lush mountains peeking over it in the background. But it also worked for investigating.

Elena stood on the sandy shoreline, a small stretch of land that the kids called 'the beach' that was almost hidden when the lake was high. Today, the lake was lower—the lowest it had been since Abby had arrived —leaving several yards of beach for the kids to make sandcastles on. Sabrina and Paxton readied canoes, each taking a pair of kids out onto the lake with them.

"Look at this," Lucas said, as he finished packing up a box of art supplies. He rattled the box with a frown. "I swear, there were thirty-two cans of paint in here, and now there's only thirty."

"I guess the kids go through them fast."

Elena took a seat in the lifeguard chair, still dressed in her thin black hoodie and jean shorts. She fidgeted with her ears, and Abby suspected she was slipping in an earbud.

"No, I haven't seen any empty," Lucas continued. "They're *missing*."

Abby was about to offer to help Lucas look under the picnic tables, when the loudspeaker crackled and an elderly woman's voice came through. "Abby Spector, please report to the main office."

Abby frowned. The message repeated once more before the loudspeaker fell silent. She turned, raising an eyebrow at Lucas.

"Go," Lucas encouraged. "I'll finish cleaning up."

"I hope you find your missing paint," Abby called back as she attempted to rub a marker stain off her hands. She turned toward the main office with curiosity.

On the outside, the main office looked like a log cabin. Except for a few large glass windows and occasional patches of stonework, it looked similar to the cabins the campers slept in.

As she approached, Jason emerged from the woods, his sleeves rolled up and sweat-stained, blond hair glistening on his damp forehead. Abby almost greeted him, but he glanced over his shoulder as if he was worried he was being followed, and her instincts told her to wait and watch. She took a small step back, disappearing around the side of the hall. Jason removed a pair of gardening gloves and wiped dried mud from his hiking boots, before heading into the main hall. Abby waited until the door slammed shut before facing the hall again.

By the time she reached the front door and stepped inside, there was no sign of Jason.

Cold air washed over Abby as she stepped into a large foyer with high ceilings, polished floors, and arched doorways. Framed pictures lined the halls—mostly of campers throughout the years. Carol sat at her desk to the right of the front door, door open to a cozy office with framed pictures and potted plants. Mina waited at the far end of the hall with a friendly wave.

Abby ran toward her, arms wide for a hug. Mina took a small step back, shaking her head, and held out a hand, gesturing down a hall to the right. "Please, follow me this way, Miss Spector."

Abby gave Mina a questioning look as Mina whispered, "I told them I had a question about your medication."

Ah. That made sense. Technically, Abby didn't have more time off than the occasional thirty-minute break, until Saturday. Mina must have had a similar grueling schedule or she would have visited Abby instead of calling her to the office. It was a good plan. This way, they could spend some uninterrupted time together.

Mina's boots thudded softly against the polished floor as she led Abby deeper down rustic halls—past a charming kitchen with wide windows and a cozy-looking library—to a barn door that squeaked as it slid open, revealing a cramped wooden room with a couch, desk, and way too many cabinets.

"What is this place?" Abby asked.

"My office," Mina explained. "They've clearly been using it for storage. Anyway, I wanted to give you this."

She picked up a thin hardback book and handed it to Abby. The smooth dark green cover and gold lettering was a near perfect match to the Camp Pine Whispers memory book that she had stuffed in a box in the back of her closet along with her old yearbooks and childhood photo albums. The difference was that this book was dated the year Cassandra went missing.

"Where did you get this?" Abby asked, cracking it open and flipping through the pages. It was in better condition than her own memory book, free from any notes, doodles, and signatures in the margins. The only signs of personalization were yellow sticky notes on several pages.

"From the library," Mina said. "I've gone through and marked everyone here this summer who was there then. It's a short list."

Abby turned to a page with a photo of Cassandra with her arms around Elena. The photo must have been taken mid-laugh, because Elena had her head back, an unusually wide grin on her face, eyes scrunched shut. It was odd to see Elena like this—younger, carefree, in a bright T-shirt and pastel shorts. As Abby's fingers brushed the page, she had a pang of sympathy for Elena. Perhaps she *was* weighed down by guilt—a similar guilt to what Abby felt for so many years. The guilt of unintentionally leading someone to their death.

That could explain why she turned to dark clothes and headphones and scowls, trying to separate herself from the rest of the world as much as possible: good old-fashioned grief mingled with unyielding remorse.

Abby imagined it must be even worse, not knowing the outcome. Not knowing if she had led Cassandra to be kidnapped or murdered or stranded in the woods. Or perhaps Elena didn't even know she had been followed that night, and thought Cassandra's disappearance had nothing to do with her.

Abby turned to the next bookmark, which marked an image of a dozen counselors waving beside the opening day sign. On the sticky note, scrawled in Mina's frilly handwriting, was a series of names: Jason, Nick, Sabrina. They had all been counselors alongside Cassandra.

She recognized Jason first, his height and blond hair making him stand out as he grinned, giving two thumbs-up, but his hair was shorter back then and he was clean-shaven. Nick was harder to spot, but she soon recognized him—he was softer, less toned, with rugged stubble and a smile that looked more like a grimace. Sabrina stood beside him—she looked like a child, with her blonde hair parted into two braids held together with butterfly clips and a rounder, softer face with a wide grin that made her eyes crinkle. Her clothes were less tailored and her left arm was wrapped in a pink cast filled with signatures.

And there, in the center of the photograph, was Cassandra, looking exactly the same as her ghost—wearing the same clothes, down to her striped socks and faded sneakers. Abby shivered, wondering if this was the last photo ever taken of her.

"Have you talked to any of them yet?" Abby asked.

Mina shook her head. "I mentioned it to Carol. I just said I heard a rumor that a counselor went missing here once and asked if it was true. She said it was unfortunate, but a freak accident. That Cassandra had taken a canoe out alone at night in the storm and likely drowned."

"Cassandra didn't say anything about a canoe," Abby pointed out.

Mina drummed her fingers on the desk. Abby was impressed she had found space between all the boxes of medical supplies and the sticky notes full of doodles or motivational quotes in Mina's handwriting. "Carol could be mistaken. Or she could be lying."

"Why would she lie?"

A floorboard squeaked as Mina adjusted her weight. "To protect herself. From incompetence or something worse."

Abby struggled to see Carol as a murderer, but if a girl had died on her campground, that would be bad for the camp's reputation. A missing girl had been bad enough. If Carol had learned about her death, could she have covered it up? "I'll ask the others and see what I can find."

Mina took Abby's hand, brushing her thumb against her wrist. "Are you sure you're up for this?"

Abby leaned into her touch, finding it soothing. She took a deep breath in. Mina's usually nutty scent was mixed with something floral—like lavender or honeysuckle. It was nice. "For helping a ghost move on? It's kind of what I'm good at."

"I know," Mina said with a look of genuine pride. "It's just—this ghost isn't someone who died hundreds of years ago. These people knew Cassandra. They could still be grieving her."

"I know." Abby gave Mina's hand a reassuring squeeze. "Are you worried?"

"I'm not worried as much as I'm...I don't know— compassionate?" Her eyes took on a faraway look. Somewhere in another part of the building, the air conditioning kicked on, its soft rattling overpowering the distant sounds of birds chirping. "I feel for these people. You know how much I hate it when strangers ask me about my mom. I'd be pretty shaken if someone started asking questions about her death, or insinuating the cancer was a cover up for murder."

"They don't know she's dead," Abby said. "They just think she's missing."

"That's got to come with its own set of emotional baggage."

"I'll be careful," Abby promised. "I'll try to be considerate."

"You know what else would be considerate?" Mina smirked, leaning in close. "If you'd stay a little longer to catch up with your girlfriend."

"Oh?" Abby asked as Mina's breath tickled her neck. "Did you want to tell me about your day?"

"I can think of better things to do with my mouth," Mina whispered. She brushed her lips across Abby's in a tender kiss that soon built into a full-on make-out session that left Abby flushed as she retreated down the hall, her lips tender and sweet with Mina's ChapStick.

Outside, the sun had sunk to the edge of the tree line, casting long shadows across the gravel parking lot. Several car-lengths away, two people were engaged in a heated discussion. Abby recognized one of them as Elena. The other had his back to her, his hair hidden under a red baseball cap. But he was broad-shouldered, muscular, and wore a camp counselor's uniform, making Abby confident it was either Paxton or Nick. Across from him, Elena's eyes were narrowed, her mouth twisted into a scowl. If it had been anyone else, Abby would have assumed they were upset, but Elena's scowl was nearly permanent.

Abby slowed down as she walked closer. Elena's scowl had grown even more menacing as the guy— Nick—unlocked the Jeep and reached inside. He pulled out a red toolbox.

Elena looked like she was about to punch him.

"Hey!" Abby called, quickening her pace. "Is everything okay?"

Elena and Nick exchanged glances. It was brief, but it told Abby that despite their disagreement, there was some underlying trust or secret between them.

"Yeah." Elena didn't even attempt to smile. "We were just catching up."

Nick grunted. "I came out here to pick up some tools and she's grilling me like I kidnapped a child."

Elena crossed her arms. "You were trying to get into Sabrina's truck."

Abby eyed the dark gray Jeep and was surprised to learn something so bland belonged to Sabrina. She would have expected her to have a small, bright-colored car, or at least a pretty keychain or cat-themed bumper stickers, but the only sign of personalization Abby could see was the fuzzy pink cover on the steering wheel.

"With keys, that she let me borrow." Nick waved the keys in front of him.

"What did you need the tools for?" Elena asked without missing a beat.

"See what I mean?" Nick gestured to Elena with exasperation. He slammed the door shut and brushed past Elena, heading back toward the cabins.

"I don't see why you can't just tell me," Elena said heatedly.

Gravel crunched under Nick's boots as he stilled and tilted his head up, shaking it like he was an exhausted parent frustrated with trying to teach a toddler to tie their shoe. He glanced back at Elena. "They're my tools. I need to make something. Happy?"

He tossed the keys into the air and caught them as

he retreated across the parking lot, the metal scattering light across dozens of car wheels.

Elena tugged on the straps of her sleeveless hoodie and slipped an earbud into one ear, then the other. "He's right, you know. We should get going." She raced down the parking lot, letting out a loud, angry breath as her black sneakers pounded the gravel, carrying her back to camp.

Chapter Seven

Abby spent the next few hours attempting to get a moment alone with Lucas. When that proved impossible, she worked with what she could realistically get.

Summer heat filled her canoe as she rowed toward Lucas, dragging Lilly and her friend along. Other campers called to one another in the distance, laughing and hollering as they raced each other with wide strokes or drifted peacefully past wildlife.

"I need your help," she called to Lucas. A breeze fluttered her life jacket, spraying her bare knees with drops of lake water that were refreshing against the humidity.

"With what?" Lucas called back, steering his canoe, and two adolescent boys, toward Abby. The boy in the front was tall and lanky, and he eagerly jammed his oar in the water, spinning the boat in circles, while the boy in the middle paled, as if he was about to be sick.

"With the investigation." Abby lowered her voice, leaning over to explain about the memory book and what had transpired between Elena and Nick as Lucas's canoe spun in slow circles. If the girls heard her, they didn't seem to mind—they were too busy scolding the boy in the front of Lucas's canoe for splashing them with his overenthusiastic strokes.

"I've been doing some digging of my own." Lucas jammed his oar between two large rocks, momentarily halting his canoe. He glanced over his shoulder and whispered, "According to an interview with Carol Silverwood, Cassandra snuck out in the middle of the night, stole a canoe, and disappeared."

"She told Mina the same thing. But Cassandra didn't say anything about a canoe."

"Well, a canoe was missing and it was found washed up on Snake Island—" Lucas nodded toward a small stretch of wilderness about the size of a soccer field in the middle of the lake. "And guess who found it?"

The boy in the front attempted to shove the canoe forward, gritting his teeth.

"Carol?" Abby considered what Mina had said about the possibility Carol had been trying to cover up a liability. She could have made up that part about the canoe to make the police think Cassandra had made a poor decision and drowned, instead of being murdered on her campground.

Lucas was shaking his head, leaning closer to Abby. He whispered, as if he was revealing the final clue to unraveling this whole thing, "*Jason.*"

Abby frowned. Jason had no reason to cover up Cassandra's death. "Why would Jason lie about that?"

"You tell me." Lucas strained as he increased his grip on his oar, keeping the canoe firmly in place. "Maybe he killed her and lied about the canoe to make it look like she ran off somewhere else. I cannot *believe* you've got us working with a murderer."

Abby held up her hand. Lucas was getting too far ahead of himself. Just because Jason claimed to have found the canoe that Cassandra had taken out didn't mean he had anything to do with her death. "We don't know he did it. Maybe he *did* find a canoe, it just wasn't Cassandra's."

"Oh, because someone else just took a midnight ride to Snake Island, abandoned the canoe, and swam back home safe and sound?"

Abby sighed. The way he put it, it did sound ridiculous. "Who else was mentioned in the article? Any of the other counselors?"

"Not by name. Just Jason and the Silverwoods."

"Including Paxton?" Abby asked, recalling that Paxton's name hadn't appeared in the memory book.

Lucas shook his head. "Just his sister."

Abby hadn't considered that there were more Silverwood kids, but she supposed they wouldn't all want to stick around here each summer. Especially if they were close with Cassandra. "What did the article say about them?"

"Carol made a statement about how much of a tragedy this was, how much Cassandra would be missed, and how the safety of the campers is Camp Pine Whispers number one priority."

"That's it?"

Lucas shrugged. "More or less. She also said that her daughter was good friends with Cassandra, and that Cassandra was like family."

"Interesting." Abby made a mental note to confirm with Cassandra that this was true and to ask Paxton for his sister's contact information.

"Of course, they're always saying all campers are like family, so I'm not sure how much weight that holds," Lucas pointed out.

The kid in the front of his boat gave up on pushing and decided to smack his oar against the water, soaking the girls in the front of Abby's boat.

"Watch it!" Lilly shouted, squeezing out her pigtails. The girl in front began to cry. Lilly scooped up a handful of water and threw it at the boy who had splashed her, coating his chin and life jacket.

"That's our cue to leave," Abby said, shoving gently away from Lucas.

"Wait!" Lucas grabbed her boat, keeping it from drifting too far. It rocked at the abrupt halt, and Abby had to grip the side to steady herself. "There's something I want you to look into for me."

"What's that?" Abby asked, following Lucas's gaze to another canoe, where Sabrina's blonde hair glistened in the sun. Her head was thrown back in laughter.

"Can you find out if she's single?" Lucas whispered.

"You haven't asked?" Abby gave him a look that said 'you're a grown man, you can ask her yourself.'

"I don't want to be creepy," Lucas replied, tightening his grip on his oar. "Just—ask her, if it comes up."

"It won't come up," Abby called back, shaking her head as she rowed away. But she made a mental note to ask the next time she talked to Sabrina. Right now, she was more concerned with talking to Paxton about his sister.

"I'm not cut out for this," Lucas called after her, reluctantly removing his oar from between the rocks. He placed it in the water and attempted to row forward. "First, these boys don't sleep. Then, they start sleeping and wake me up in the middle of the night complaining about shadows. Or imaginary raccoons. And what's worse, someone keeps stealing my art supplies."

"I'm sure no one is stealing your art supplies," Abby had to raise her voice to reach him as she drifted further from his canoe, which was spinning in slow circles.

"They are," Lucas protested. "I've counted and labeled everything and—"

Splash.

The water surged, rocking Abby's canoe so hard it nearly toppled. The girls gasped. Abby stifled a laugh as the boy who had previously been in the front of Lucas's canoe now spluttered in the water, bobbing up and down on his life jacket. He flailed his arms before grabbing hold of Lucas's canoe.

"That's what you get for trying to splash people," Lucas said, cautiously scooting forward and reaching for the boy.

The boy grabbed his arm and pulled. Lucas gave a startled cry before he tumbled into the lake after him. He soon broke the surface, glasses askew and dripping, glaring so hard he rivaled Elena.

Abby suppressed a grin as she navigated the boat back to shore. It was only water. Lucas would dry off and be fine in no time. The girls had popsicles to eat. And she had an investigation to conduct.

PAXTON WAS SURPRISINGLY easy to locate—in the lifeguard chair—his usual clothes replaced with red swim trunks and a white tank that revealed a clear tan line from his watch. Neither of her campers complained about returning to shore early as they had first pick of popsicles from the cooler. Once they were happily indulging in their treats on the beach, Abby picked up two extra popsicles and headed in Paxton's direction. She extended them toward him. "Take your pick."

Sun gleamed off Paxton's sunglasses as he considered a moment before reaching for the blue one. "Thanks."

Abby opened the remaining popsicle and leaned casually against the lifeguard stand. It was hard to believe his highlights were natural. They were perfectly golden against his otherwise brown hair. Abby was only a little jealous that all this sun made her own hair messy and brittle, while Paxton's looked soft and wavy, like he could be the lead actor in one of those beachy romantic comedies. "Do you have actual lifeguard training or are you just really good at swimming?"

Paxton smirked. "Both."

"Have you ever had to save anyone?" Abby tried to approach the subject casually. "Any campers? Siblings?"

"I'm an only child," Paxton said. "And no, thankfully. There've been a few near accidents, but by the time I reach the water the kid is fine."

"But the articles said you have a sister," Abby said, unable to stop herself. Lucas would not have gotten such a crucial detail wrong. She instantly regretted her tone when it occurred to her that Paxton's sister could have died.

Paxton glanced quizzically at Abby before returning his gaze to the lake, where the other canoes began to drift to shore. "What articles?"

Abby tried to think of a way to bring up her interest in Cassandra's death that didn't come off creepy. "A counselor, Cassandra, died here a few years ago. We'd been campers together a few years before. So I read the articles about her death."

Paxton finished the rest of his popsicle in three swift bites and folded the wrapper between his thumbs, his gaze never leaving the water. Waves lapped against the shore as birds circled in the cloudless sky.

Abby continued cautiously. "It would have been nice to talk to someone else who misses her."

A sliver of guilt prickled Abby's stomach at the lie, but it wasn't entirely untrue. She *was* Cassandra's friend —she had just left off the part about having had the majority of their conversations *after* her death. Now all she could do was wait and hope Paxton offered something more about Cassandra.

Abby had all but written off this conversation as a dead end and was starting to turn away when Paxton said softly, "I miss her too."

"You knew her?" It shouldn't have come as a surprise considering Cassandra had attended camp for years, and Paxton was likely around at least some of those years.

He nodded. "We were best friends. I hadn't transitioned yet."

Oh. Abby's cheeks warmed with embarrassment at having not considered that Paxton could be trans. The thought hadn't even crossed her mind. "I'm sorry for assuming—"

"It's okay. Pretty much everyone here knows, and they're cool with it. I'm lucky that I have such a supportive place here." Paxton leaned forward. "You wanted to talk about Cass?"

"Yeah," Abby said, trying to get her thoughts together. Now that she knew Paxton had been there that summer, he had suddenly become a suspect. She needed to tread more carefully. "I just…can't believe she died."

"She didn't die." Paxton turned his gaze back to the lake, running a hand through his tousled hair, his expression hidden behind those damn sunglasses. "She ran away. And I don't blame her."

Chapter Eight

Abby studied Paxton to see if there were any signs that he truly believed what he was saying or if he was lying—if he knew what had happened to Cassandra and didn't want anyone to find out. Unable to come to a conclusion, she pressed, "Why would she run away?"

Paxton let out a heavy sigh. "Things were tough that summer. Cass and I had just graduated high school. We had big plans—go to college together, win the National Swim Championships, maybe run this place together one day. At least, those were my plans. I thought she was on the same page. But the week before she ran away was different. She was worried about something. She wouldn't tell me what. And that was unusual—we told each other *everything*. I thought it might have had something to do with Nick."

"Nick—is this the same Nick that's a counselor here?"

Paxton nodded. "They'd dated, briefly, senior year, and broken up right before camp started. But after she went missing, a lot of stuff came to light that had me rethinking that summer."

Abby couldn't help but think about going through Chelsea's room after she had died—the bittersweet pang that came with learning something new, like how she collected soda bottle caps in her nightstand and had a printed copy of sappy *Once Upon a Time* fanfiction under her bed. It made Chelsea feel simultaneously closer and far away.

Abby could only imagine how those feelings would become even more complex if she hadn't known what had happened to Chelsea, or if she'd learned some dark secret. "What kind of stuff?"

Paxton shrugged. "Personal stuff. Family stuff. Like, Cass told me she put my name down to be roommates at App State—but it turned out she deferred going to college."

"And you didn't find out until after she went missing?"

Paxton shook his head. "Apparently, she told her mom she was planning on staying home, taking classes at the local community college. But all that time, she must have been planning on running away."

Abby chewed her lip. If Cassandra had been planning on running away, she hadn't gotten very far. And if she hadn't—would learning of her plans have upset someone enough to kill her? "What do you think she was trying to escape?"

"Who knows. Family problems, money problems…" His voice trailed off and Abby sensed that he had stopped himself from saying something more. He fidgeted with the rope of the whistle around his neck. He blew it once, a sharp, piercing sound that signaled it was time for break.

The kids scrambled from the water, splashing each other as they made their way to shore. Abby sensed her time for questioning coming to an end. She concluded by asking, "What about Elena? Were she and Cassandra close?"

"They had their ups and downs, as any family does."

Abby did a double take. "Elena's related to Cassandra?"

"They were sisters." Paxton descended the lifeguard stand and propped up a 'no swimming' sign. "Technically, stepsisters. Their parents divorced a few months before camp. Elena had a really hard time when Cass left. We all did, but Elena might have had the hardest time of all of us."

"By 'all of us,' you mean you, Nick, Elena, and—?"

"I mean out of *all of us*." Paxton turned to Abby, a darkening expression on his face. "Everyone who was there that summer. We all miss Cass. She really was like family. But for Elena, she was *actually* family."

Sounds of joy and laughter rose a few yards away as a group of kids began a game of volleyball. Paxton started toward them, signaling the conversation was over.

Abby called after him, "If her disappearance was so hard on everyone, why come back each summer?"

He turned back to her, finally lowering his sunglasses, revealing stormy blue eyes and a pained expression. "Because this is where we feel closest to her. I think a part of us hopes that maybe, just maybe, we'll wake up one morning and find she's returned."

Abby wanted to share a word of encouragement, but she knew it wasn't true. Cassandra was never coming back. At least not alive.

"You believe Paxton?" Mina's bracelets clattered as she rested her elbows against the picnic blanket, letting the sun kiss her shoulders, her athletic shorts wrinkling around her waist. Sun glistened off her kicked-off sandals that lay beside a wicker basket at the corner of the blanket, her bare feet pointed at the lake. Abby loved seeing her like this, so relaxed and peaceful.

She and Chelsea had gone to the beach once—she remembered Chelsea's green swimsuit and her enthusiastic laugh as she cannonballed off the pier. She could no longer remember how her lips tasted or the exact feeling of her embrace, but she knew it had felt like a firework—bright and thrilling and over too soon. Mina's presence was different—warm and cozy, as if it were a clear sunrise after a stormy night.

"I think so," Abby admitted, turning up the volume of the walkie-talkie at her side. "I wanted to talk to Cassandra but it doesn't seem like she plans on making an appearance."

"This is where you saw her last?"

"On that hill." Abby tilted her head toward the path where she had last seen Cassandra. The path was too narrow for a picnic, and the space on top of the cliffside was too overgrown. Luckily, this sandy lakeside clearing was just around the bend, offering Abby a good view of the spots where Cassandra had appeared, while also serving as a romantic getaway.

Mina shrugged, reaching for a bottle of lemonade. "Her loss, my win."

Abby grinned, meeting Mina's lips in an endearing kiss. "Very true."

Mina nodded to the darkening clouds drifting over the lake. "We should eat before it rains."

She slipped a pair of sandwiches from the wicker picnic basket complete with the Camp Pine Whispers logo across the red lining.

"How come I didn't get one of those?" Abby asked, taking her egg salad sandwich. All she had gotten was a flannel blanket that was way too hot to use this time of year.

"I borrowed it from the Lodge."

"What do I need to do to get a room there?" Abby teased.

"A nursing degree. Or whatever fancy degree the program and hiring directors have. Or be related to the owners."

"Paxton stays there?" Her mind conjured an image of Paxton in some fancy bedroom with strong AC and tons of outlets, staring out the window at a gorgeous view of the campgrounds.

"He has a room over mine." Mina cradled her

lemonade like a beer bottle as she reached for a bag of pretzels. "He plays the guitar, you know. At first, I thought it would be awful, but he's good at stopping before it gets too late and he's not a bad player."

"Does he seem trustworthy to you?"

Mina tapped the bottle as she considered the question. Her fingernails were painted like the night sky, with swirling constellations. Impressive, as always. "I don't know him well enough to say either way. If you can't reach Cassandra, you could corroborate his story with Elena and Nick."

"Corroborate whose story?" a voice asked softly.

Abby scrambled to turn up the walkie-talkie. She grabbed the binoculars and saw Cassandra in her eerily dated camp uniform, standing at the edge of the lake.

"Paxton," Abby explained. "Paxton Silverwood— but you probably didn't know him by that name. His parents own this place. The articles said you were best friends."

Cassandra blinked.

Abby continued, "He's trans. He's a guy now."

"I get it." Cassandra glanced down at the lake. "I'm just— processing. So much has changed. But Paxton— is happy?"

"I think so," Abby said.

Cassandra turned back to her and nodded. "Good. Paxton's a good name. It suits him. What did you want to know?"

Abby shifted her weight awkwardly. "Well, he seems to be under the impression that you ran away."

Cassandra folded her arms across her chest. "Why would he think that?"

"He says that some information came out after you went missing—well, died, but he doesn't know that. He wasn't specific. Just said family stuff, personal stuff, and something about college and plans being different."

Cassandra sat, forming a triangle between the three of them.

"I never wanted it to be like this. Paxton and I had plans for college, but I don't think he realized how hard it was for me. Sure, I got in, I got a scholarship. But it wasn't a full ride. My mom was going through a divorce, and she was…not in a good place. She needed help. Elena needed help. I couldn't leave them, I just couldn't. I was going to tell Paxton. Please, tell him I had plans to visit, and to enroll the following year."

Abby glanced uncertainly at Mina, who gave an unhelpful 'don't look at me' shrug. She turned back to Cassandra's pleading face and said carefully, "Paxton thinks you're still alive. Do you want me to tell him otherwise?"

Cassandra turned back to the lake once more, as if she were searching for Paxton. It was strange to watch the breeze drift right through her, without loosening a single braid. "Can I speak with him?"

Abby's stomach knotted. While she would love to avoid having to break the news to Paxton, and she would do anything to help Cassandra, she didn't think inviting a potential murder suspect to chat was the best course of action. "Once we figured out what happened to you, you can talk to anyone you want to. I'll help."

Cassandra stared at a patch of wildflowers, seeming to think it over. "Trust Paxton. He wouldn't have killed me."

Abby accepted this with an open mind. After all, Chelsea would have sworn Abby had nothing to do with her death, but she had everything to do with it. Paxton may never have intended to kill Cassandra, but that didn't mean he was innocent. "What about your ex-boyfriend?"

"Nick?" Cassandra leaned back, letting out a heavy sigh. "No, he wouldn't hurt me. He cares about me— or he did. I suppose he's probably moved on by now."

Abby chewed her lip. She didn't recall Nick wearing a wedding ring, but that didn't mean he was single. She glanced at Mina, a nasty swell of emotions rising in the pit of her stomach as she imagined what Chelsea would think of her if her ghost were here. She hoped she would be happy for her, but doubt crept in as she recalled Chelsea's occasional jealousy about her spending so much time with Lucas.

Mina took advantage of the silence and asked gently, "Can you think of anyone we *should* be suspicious of?"

"The Brazen Brushstrokes," Cassandra said instantly. "They were a group Elena met up with— artists for activism, but the things they were doing were getting more and more dangerous: graffitiing streets, churches, government property. The police were after them. They had traced a few leads back to the summer camp. I think Elena was going to meet up with them that night—I warned her not to, but she never listens. Someone from that group could have done it."

"Do you know anyone else who was in it?"

Cassandra shook her head. "Not by name, but I know they were art students from Brevard College."

"We'll look into it." Abby made a mental note to ask Lucas to see if any of the counselors that summer had been students at Brevard. "What about Sabrina?"

Cassandra shook her head. "Sabrina and I taught basket-weaving together. She was quiet, good with the kids. I liked her. She was in a car accident a few weeks ago—well, a few weeks before I…died."

"Is that how she broke her arm?" Abby asked, recalling the cast she wore in the memory book photograph.

Cassandra nodded. "I felt bad for her. She seemed really stressed. I got the sense her dad wasn't a nice man. He was really upset about the car."

Abby was taken aback. She couldn't imagine being upset about a car after a loved one survived a car accident. She tried not to picture the sirens and police officers that had arrived after Chelsea's death. "Was the accident her fault?"

"There was a storm," Cassandra said with a shrug, as if to say she didn't know. "She hit a tree. She wasn't drunk or anything, if that's what you're asking. But the car was totaled. And she walked away."

Cassandra traced her wrist as if wishing that she could have traded her fate for Sabrina's. Abby cleared her throat, wanting to move away from the subject of car accidents. "And Jason?"

"Jason had this whole 'man of the wilderness' vibe going on."

"He still does."

Cassandra nodded as if that didn't surprise her. "We weren't particularly close. He was just this goofy guy, you know? Always messing around, not really taking anything seriously. I don't exactly trust him, but I don't have anything against him."

"And Carol Silverwood," Mina supplied. "What about her?"

"The Silverwoods were like family to me," Cassandra said. "They would never have hurt me."

"I believe that," said Abby. "But if they learned after the fact that you had died on their property, and they thought it was an accident, would they have covered it up? Was there any reason that they wouldn't want people to know what happened?"

"No." Cassandra rose, balling her fists at her side. Her hair began to billow in a rising wind that emanated from her core. Despite the sun on Abby's shoulders, cold prickled the back of her neck.

Cassandra's voice boomed through the walkie-talkie. "It *wasn't* the Silverwoods. It was one of the fake activists. Or a stranger. A serial killer or something like that. There were rumors, you know, of a man who had gotten lost in the woods and wandered around so long his clothes rotted away."

Chills spread deeper down Abby's spine. She glanced over her shoulder, expecting some shadowy figure to jump out at any moment. She pictured such a figure murdering Cassandra, taking a canoe, and fleeing to Snake Island. Suppressing a shudder, she offered, "On the night you died, they found a canoe. They thought it was yours."

Cassandra stiffened. "It wasn't. I didn't go near the canoes that night."

"That's what we thought," Abby said with a sigh.

Mina put a comforting hand on her shoulder. "It sounds like we've got work to do."

Chapter Nine

Wind whispered through the trees as Abby returned to camp, the sprinkling rain causing goosebumps to prickle her bare arms. She found it refreshing after such a hot day, and took her time meandering back to the cabin.

Elena's voice boomed as Abby cracked open the door and shuffled inside—she was reading from a book of children's stories, competing with the rattling fan and growing storm. The campers listened eagerly, perched on the edge of their bright sleeping bags or on well-worn pillows on the floor. A few of them glanced up at Abby's arrival. Lilly waved and Abby returned the gesture as she unlaced her damp sneakers.

Elena shut the book mid-sentence, earning cries of protest.

"It's Abby's turn now," she said dryly, grabbing her black hoodie from the side of her bed. She pulled it over her T-shirt and it jingled with the sound of keys. "I'll be right back."

Abby eyed her suspiciously. "Where are you going?"

"On a murder spree."

Rain pattered against the window, heightening the tension between them. A crooked grin passed over Elena's face, as if she took pride in making Abby uncomfortable.

"It was a joke, jeez." Elena rolled her eyes and stepped past Abby, slipping into a pair of black rain boots.

Abby took a moment to compose herself. Elena sounded casual, but she couldn't shake the feeling that her previous comment had been a threat. She cleared her throat. "I actually hoped we could find some time to talk."

"What about?"

Abby glanced at the kids, who were watching this exchange as if it were a reality TV show. Some were staring, entranced, shoving handfuls of popcorn into their mouths. "Something we should discuss in private."

Elena gave a noncommittal shrug, picked up an umbrella, and shoved open the door. Wind rushed into the cabin, rain splattering the doorstep as Elena stepped out and gestured for Abby to follow.

Abby glanced back at the kids. "Now?"

"When else do you expect to have time?"

Hesitantly, Abby stepped onto the front porch and shut the door behind her. A heavy gust of wind poured rain across her bare feet and she shivered, folding her arms across her T-shirt as goosebumps trailed her legs.

Elena moved further toward the top of the front steps, her dark hair battering her face as she turned to Abby expectantly. "Well?"

Abby had waited for this moment for so long, but now that it was here, she wished she had thought of the best way to broach the subject. "I'm not sure how to ask this. It's about Cassandra."

Elena stiffened. "What about her?"

"The night she went missing, she was worried about you. She thought you were meeting up with some group. The Brazen Brushstrokes?"

Elena's eyes flashed. "Who told you this? Was it Nick?"

"Cassandra did."

Elena eyed her intensely. Abby wasn't sure if she believed her or not, but she continued, "I think she might have snuck out that night—the night she went missing—to follow you."

Elena gave a harsh, bitter laugh. It resonated with anguish and disbelief, sending a stab of pain through Abby's chest. She hated making Elena relive such a dark memory.

Elena's expression hardened with cold denial. "You want to know what happened to her? Get in line. We've been over it with the police a hundred times. They say she ran away."

"But you don't believe them?"

"No." Rain pounded harder, falling in sheets now,

accompanied by the distant roar of thunder. Elena leaned in, lowering her voice. "She's dead."

Abby sucked in a breath. "How can you be so sure?"

Elena pulled her hood over her head and opened her umbrella with a *snap*. Abby half expected her to declare that she had witnessed her murder—or worse, that she had killed her. But her voice softened as she said, "Because if she was still alive, she would have reached out."

Without another glance at Abby, she stepped out into the storm and faded into the darkening horizon.

It was nearly an hour before Elena returned and carefully removed her rain boots without a word about where she had been. The storm was letting up, the rain reduced to hardly a drizzle. Elena explained calmly that the girls were to form two lines as Abby and Elena accompanied them to the main hall for arts and crafts.

Abby's chaperone duties did not let up until after dinner, when she spent the evening in her bunk, hiding under her covers with a flashlight, contemplating her list of suspects and the best questions to ask Cassandra when her spirit returned. Getting nowhere, she pivoted to making a list of questions for Paxton. In minutes, she had over a dozen questions about the night Cassandra went missing. The challenge was finding a way to phrase these questions that didn't make *her* sound suspicious. No matter how she approached them, she couldn't think of a way to bring up murder in casual conversation.

It was nearly midnight before her eyelids grew heavy. One of her final thoughts as she drifted off to sleep was how much easier this would be if she could get the other counselors to talk to Cassandra's ghost.

"You want to *what?*" Lucas asked, his voice hitching.

"Shh!" Abby brought her finger to her lips, gesturing toward the dozens of campers playing volleyball on the sunlit beach. Sabrina gave her and Lucas a curious glance before blowing a whistle and enforcing a break on a rather heated volleyball match.

"I'm sorry," Lucas said, lowering his voice. "But in what world do you think it'd be a good idea to go up to someone and say 'Hey, you know your friend who died a few years ago? Her ghost is hanging out in the woods, want to see?'"

"I won't say it like that," Abby protested. Over the past few days, the idea had remained in her mind, growing more and more feasible each day. "I have a plan. I'll ask Paxton for his help, lead him into the woods, turn on the walkie-talkie, and let Cassandra do the rest."

Lucas shook his head. "You are going to scare the guy to death."

"Come on, you know if I had the chance to talk to Chelsea again, I'd take it."

Lucas leaned back, squinting against the sun as he

met her gaze. Abby could tell he wanted to say some-thing, but he shook his head, holding himself back.

"What?" Abby asked.

"Nothing."

"I know that look. Whatever you want to say, I can handle it. Just tell me."

Lucas rubbed his chin. "Okay. I know you miss Chelsea. You didn't get closure when she died. It was sudden, unexpected—tragic. I get why you want to find her. But if you do manage to contact her spirit? I'm worried it would just make things worse."

Abby's muscles tightened. "What could be worse than Chelsea being dead?"

Lucas winced, but he didn't miss a beat as he said, "You spiraling back into depression—or latching onto her spirit and trying to keep her around until you realize she wasn't as amazing as you keep thinking she was."

Abby stared at him in stunned silence. A powerful gust of wind sent sand hurling against her legs. "You didn't like Chelsea?"

Lucas licked his lips and leaned forward, resting his elbows on the picnic table. "She was great. That's not the point."

But he had hesitated too long. She folded her arms across her chest. "Then why did you say it?"

"I was speculating. The point is—I'd be worried about you reuniting with Chelsea. Imagine if she'd been missing all this time and you discovered that not only has she been dead the past ten years, but she was also murdered and one of your friends may have had something to do with it." He took a deep breath. "That's what you'd be springing on Paxton."

Paxton's boisterous laugh carried over the rustling leaves and gently lapping waves. He was leading a dozen or so campers through another round of volleyball, leaving Sabrina to lounge on a picnic blanket and flip through a magazine. Abby considered Lucas's words, trying to imagine how much heartbreak she'd be putting Paxton through—but her thoughts were stuck on that phrase: *she wasn't as amazing as you keep thinking she was.*

When Abby had first met Chelsea, she spent many nights staying up late telling Lucas all about her. He'd offered her nothing but encouragement. Had she missed some secret resentment?

"Abby—" Lucas began, his voice tight with concern.

"I'm fine," Abby assured him, shoving back from the picnic table.

Lilly ran up to Abby, breathing hard, waving a life jacket. For a moment, Abby feared someone was drowning, but then Lilly exclaimed, "I want to go boating!"

Abby's heart rate returned to a normal pace as she glanced toward the canoes that remained on shore and the distant figures of several other campers who had gone further out. Helping Lily was something she could focus on, a problem she could solve. "Do you have someone to go with you?"

"Samantha and Amy," Lilly said proudly, pointing to two girls who stood by a paddle boat, yellow life jackets gleaming in the sun. Lilly held up her life jacket. "But it's broke."

"*Broken*," Lucas corrected.

Abby shot him an annoyed look. Why did he have to act like he knew *everything*?

Lilly scrunched up her nose. "No, it's still *broke*."

Lucas looked as if he was about to go into a lecture about grammar, so Abby said quickly, "Let's see if I can fix it."

Her knees met warm sand as she knelt to examine Lilly's orange life jacket. Within seconds, it was clear the upper clasp was broken. That would not be easily fixed.

"Let's get you a new life jacket," Abby said, guiding Lilly toward the boat shed. She attempted to open the door, but it was locked.

"Wait here a minute." Abby walked toward the volleyball game, waving to get Paxton's attention. The ball switched hands three times before soaring over Sabrina and rolling to a stop beside the picnic tables.

As Paxton jogged to retrieve it, Abby intercepted him, holding up Lilly's damaged life jacket. "Do you have a key to the shed?"

"Sure." Paxton removed a ring of keys from his pocket and tossed it to Abby. There were over a dozen keys on it. He resumed jogging and called, "It's the small bronze one."

"Thanks!" Abby found the key in question and returned to the shed, where Lilly bounced eagerly on her feet.

"Is that guy just handing out keys now?" Lucas asked.

"To people he trusts," Abby said heatedly, feeling a rising frustration at Lucas's presence. "I'm clearly trustworthy. Right?"

The door creaked open into a long, narrow shed. The sun only illuminated the first two or three feet. Abby removed her phone from her back pocket and turned on the flashlight, stepping inside.

"That depends," Lucas replied, leaning against the doorway. "I trust you with a lot of things. Keeping track of keys isn't one of them."

Abby tried to turn back to glare at him, but it was too cramped to easily turn around, so she settled for craning her neck momentarily before moving deeper ahead. The sides of the shack were lined with oars, canoes, kayaks, and paddleboards of all shapes and sizes, as well as several trunks of boating supplies.

Behind her, Lilly's teeth chattered. "It's creepy in here."

Abby agreed. There was something off-putting about its cold, stuffy silence. She opened the nearest trunk, and found it crammed with oars. The second was full of water shoes and ponchos. The third, an odd collection of trinkets—old watches, buttons, jewelry. This must be where they stored lost and found objects. Some of these had definitely seen better days. The watches looked ancient.

A string of pearls caught the light of Abby's phone and she was reaching toward it, lost in the memory of Chelsea waving around a pearl necklace her grandmother had given her for Christmas, declaring she felt like she was on the *Titanic*. She'd joked that maybe the weight of the pearls had caused the ship to sink. Abby remembered laughing, thinking how wonderful they looked around her neck. But now she wondered if she would laugh at that same joke, knowing how many lives were lost. Is that what Lucas didn't like about her, her sense of humor?

"Life jackets!" Lilly exclaimed gleefully, slipping past Abby, deeper into the shed. Abby shut the box and followed to a pile of life jackets crammed between a stack of kickboards and an old wardrobe.

Abby sorted through them until she found one that fit snugly over Lilly's arms. She clasped the straps across Lilly's chest and waist, earning a gleeful shout from Lilly.

"What are you doing here?" Nick's voice called from behind.

"Abby's getting Lilly a working life jacket," Lucas replied.

Abby turned carefully—but not carefully enough. Her elbow knocked into something hard behind a plastic tarp and she winced, rubbing the spot as she followed Lilly back between the overflowing boxes.

Nick pointed at Lilly. "For future reference, campers aren't allowed in here. Walls aren't finished. Some poor kid stepped on a nail once. It was a nightmare."

"I'll keep that in mind," Abby said, halting the massage on her bruised elbow long enough to turn off her flashlight as she stepped out into the sun.

Nick shut the door behind her, locking it with his own bronze key, before walking back toward his cabin. How come he got a key and she didn't?

Abby turned to Lucas to voice this thought, then remembered she was mad at him. She held up the heavy key ring. "Guess I should give these back."

"You should," Lucas agreed.

Abby hesitated, sunlight sparkling off dozens of metal keys that promised her access to an untold number of secrets.

"Abby?" Lucas asked with concern. "What are you thinking?"

"I'm thinking you should ask Sabrina to take you out in the canoe," Abby said to Lilly. "Lucas and I have work to do."

Chapter Ten

Abby ignored Lucas's protests as she unlocked the main office. He still followed her inside.

"What are we doing here?" He peeked through the blinds as if he expected someone to return any second.

"Looking for clues."

"Right, but what exactly do you think you'll find?"

"I don't know," Abby admitted, shuffling through bills and various forms on Carol's desk. She tried to focus on the documents in front of her, but her mind kept drifting back to Chelsea and her pearl necklace. "Was it her sense of humor?"

"What?"

"Chelsea. Did you not like her sense of humor? Was it too dark for you?"

"Jesus, Abby, focus!" Lucas turned to give her an incredulous look before returning to his post at the window. "What are you looking for?"

"Something about Cassandra." Abby attempted to

open the top drawer, but found it locked. She reached for Paxton's keys and tried them one at a time. "You didn't answer my question."

"Look, look," he said excitedly. Too excitedly. Either there was a celebrity outside the front door or he wanted to divert Abby's attention. "Jason's coming out of the woods with a shovel and— Is that a toolbox? Why would he need a toolbox on a hike?"

Hating that his distraction was working, Abby forced herself not to hurry to his side, instead meandering slowly to join him at the window. She had to lift a blind to see more than the glow of sunlight, and it took her eyes a moment to adjust to the brightness. Sure enough, Jason soon came into view, his T-shirt damp with sweat, his cargo pants stained with dirt. Sunlight glistened off the metal shovel slung over his shoulders and winked across the handle of the red toolbox in his grip.

Abby frowned. "That's Nick's toolbox."

"How do you know?"

"I've seen it before."

"It's a generic toolbox. There's probably a bunch of them around here."

Abby didn't like to think that he was right, but Nick had loaned his toolbox to Sabrina, so it was reasonable he would loan it to Jason as well. And while she admitted she was intrigued by what he would need a toolbox for in the woods, she was more intrigued by what secrets about Cassandra were locked in Carol's office.

"You didn't answer my question." Abby let go of

the blinds, letting them snap back in place as she returned to the drawer. She selected a key at random and sighed when it didn't fit.

"What question?"

"About Chelsea," Abby said, trying yet another wrong key. "What didn't you like about her?"

"I liked Chelsea, okay. I just said she wasn't perfect." His strong hand rested gently on her elbow as he directed her away from the drawer. She gripped the handle, refusing to budge.

He pursed his lips. "Cassandra went missing ten years ago. Anything about her would be in storage or on there." He pointed at Carol's computer.

A slideshow of camp photos scrolled across the screen. Abby chewed her lip. Lucas was probably right, but she didn't want to admit it. She tried the final two keys on Paxton's keyring, just to be sure. When the drawer didn't budge, she moved to the computer and clicked the mouse. The screensaver was replaced by a bright password page. She tried a series of numbers that she had read were the most common passwords when she had tried to get into her mom's iPad as a teenager. None of them worked.

"You're going to get her account locked," Lucas said.

"Do you have any suggestions?"

"I'm not helping you break into someone's computer." Lucas snapped his head away from her, as if making a point. Without looking back, he called, "Try Paxton."

Abby followed his suggestion and the password

screen peeled back, revealing the desktop. She whooped in triumph, but fell quiet as Lucas shushed her.

Now there was a series of folders to navigate—Marketing Copy, Financial Information, Camper Registration—but nothing stood out as relevant.

"Search for a folder with the year you want," Lucas offered, "2015."

Abby did as instructed, and opened the folder to find dozens of additional folders stored inside. One included 'Missing Person: Cassandra Burke.' She mentally thanked Carol for such efficient organization.

Dozens of files opened up—police reports, images, witness statements, documented transcripts. Abby clicked through them, one by one, Lucas hovering on her shoulder as she pieced together the story from that night: Cassandra had gone to bed. In the middle of the night, sometime between 10 p.m. and 4 a.m., she had snuck out, gotten into a canoe, and vanished. A thunderstorm hit around midnight, and gradually retreated until sunrise. The police had never found her body. The investigation had been halted three days later when a more vicious storm caused significant damage to the surrounding area.

There was a document of statements and tips from people who had called or emailed after the event. Some of them were dated three years later. Abby's hopes fell as she realized they were unhelpful—a boy woken up twice in the middle of the night as the door opened and shut to his cabin, and two girls with a similar story—but finally, there was a statement that made Abby's breath catch: *I went to the bathroom in the middle of the night. I think it was around midnight. It was raining, but not too hard. I remember hearing a door close. I saw someone leave cabin three or four. I didn't think anything of it. I thought they were just going to the bathroom like I was. But with everything that happened, if it helps—they were wearing a black hoodie.*

Abby instantly pictured Elena in her signature black hoodie, the hood pulled over her dark hair. This was proof that she had left that night. Cassandra wasn't the only one who had seen her.

The front door rattled, opening and closing with a click. The soft thud of hiking boots echoed down the hall, growing louder.

"Someone's coming!" Lucas's voice hitched.

"I've got this," Abby assured him, closing out everything on Carol's computer. "How do I get the screensaver to come back up?"

Lucas flashed her a look that was both annoyed and frantic as he took over, quickly pulling up the screensaver. No sooner had his finger left the mouse than the door creaked open. Carol stepped inside, blinking in surprise. "What are you doing in here?"

Abby held up the keys. "Just dropping these off. Paxton let me borrow them to get something out of the shed. I wasn't sure where he was, so I figured I'd leave them here. I trust you'll be able to give them back to him?"

"Oh, of course," Carol said, her face brightening. "That's no problem. Thanks, Abby."

Abby gave her a friendly wave as they passed, which hopefully distracted her from Lucas's quiet strangled sound. When the door shut behind them, Lucas turned to Abby and whispered, "I'm never doing that again. What did we even get out of that?"

"Not as much as I'd hoped," Abby admitted. "But it proved that we're onto something. The police weren't able to find out what happened to Cassandra because they didn't have her side of the story."

"Or her body," Lucas pointed out. "Or any evidence that was lost in the storm."

"We don't have that either," Abby reminded him. "But we have Cassandra. And half a dozen people who were there with her that summer. If we can get them to talk to her, the full story is bound to come to light."

Lucas let out a deep breath. "I don't like this plan. But I can't think of anything better."

"You're on board?"

He nodded, heightening Abby's resolve. "I'm on board."

Chapter Eleven

Abby waited in Mina's room until rain splattered the window, muffling the guitar music that drifted from above, signaling Paxton was home. She put on her rain jacket, grabbed Mina's water bottle, and sprinkled some water on her head to make it look like she had been out in the rain.

Mina's lips curled with a hint of amusement. "You could just walk outside, you know."

Abby shook her head. "I can't risk running into him in the hall. Remember, if he knocks on your door, you aren't here."

Mina's oversized flannel drooped down her shoulder as she folded her arms across her tank top. It was one of her favorite flannels—a deep indigo and white, with a single butterfly patch embroidered over the heart. It was soft and faded—and had been since the first time Abby had seen Mina wear it. She'd seen her put it on at least a dozen times since, especially on days when she was nervous about a particular stunt or disappointed that one she had been looking forward to had been pulled at the last minute. Abby had even snuggled into it a few times herself, finding it cozy and warm when they were lounging in bed together, or when she made Mina's coffee in the morning while Mina slept in.

"Let's hope I don't lose my job for this."

"You won't," Abby reassured her, placing a comforting hand on Mina's arm. Paxton would realize one way or another that Abby's cry for help was fake. As long as Cassandra showed up, he wouldn't blame her for lying. "I really appreciate you doing this."

"You owe me." Mina's lips curved into a flirtatious smile.

"I can't wait to pay," Abby replied, returning her smile as a few sweet—and a few rather naughty—ideas crossed her mind. She lifted herself onto her toes as Mina leaned down, meeting her in a kiss that tasted of ChapStick and coffee; it was over too soon.

"Hurry up and come back," Mina whispered, repositioning her flannel over her shoulders.

Abby nodded. Before she could get too carried away in her fantasies, she stepped into the hallway and took a deep breath. It was time to focus. This *had* to work.

Her footsteps echoed across the creaky stairs as she hurried to the top floor and pounded on Paxton's door. Even if Mina hadn't told her its location, the sign reading 'Paxton' was a dead giveaway.

The door opened almost instantly. Paxton stood in

the doorway, a guitar hanging over his dark green camp counselor T-shirt and gray sweatpants. He blinked in confusion.

"I need your help," Abby said, putting her acting skills to the test. "Lucas sprained his ankle."

"Did you take him to the nurse?" Paxton asked.

Abby shook her head. "Mina's out. I didn't know where to go, so I came to you."

Paxton ran his hands through his hair. "I'm not a doctor…"

"We don't need a doctor," Abby said, thinking quickly. "Not yet. He's in the woods. He can't walk, but he's conscious. The two of us could probably support him enough, he could hobble back here."

"I think there's a pair of crutches in the storage closet," Paxton said, reaching for his keys. "I broke my foot a few years ago. Let's hope Mom hasn't given them away."

Abby couldn't think of a reason to protest this without giving away her act, so she waited nervously in the hallway while Paxton unlocked the door across the hall and disappeared in the walk-in closet. She could hear him rummaging around over the wind's rising howl.

At last, he emerged with a pair of dusty crutches. He held them up triumphantly before handing them to Abby.

"Maybe you could come with me?" Abby suggested. "In case he needs help. Or we get lost. I'm terrible with directions."

Paxton raised an eyebrow as he returned to his

room. He reached for a rain jacket hanging near the door. "Can you at least remember your way back to him?"

Abby ensured the walkie-talkie was turned on and tucked safely under her rain jacket as they entered the damp woods. It was the perfect excuse to pretend Lucas had the other half of a set, and that they would know when they got close because he would hear them.

Gentle rain splattered leaves and slipped down tree trunks to pool in mossy beds. Abby felt surprisingly few drops against her rain jacket while they trudged through the thickest part of the forest, Paxton's flashlight bouncing along the trail ahead. It was more comforting than necessary as the woods were dim and gray.

"Lucas!" Paxton cupped his hands around his mouth and shouted, "Can you hear us?"

As they neared the area where Abby had first come across Cassandra, she raised the binoculars, careful to cup her hands over the top, preventing more than a few raindrops from landing on them.

Through the lenses, the forest took on an even grayer tone, with ghosts of trees long since dead covering the now living branches. But no Cassandra.

"There," Paxton called, pointing to several footprints in a damp patch of dirt to the side of the path. They headed off the trail, into the woods.

"Lucas wouldn't have left the path," Abby said. The

clearing she had last seen Cassandra in was only a few yards ahead. She didn't want to get sidetracked, but she was curious as to who was wandering off the path so near Cassandra's spot. And more importantly, why.

Paxton was already rushing into the undergrowth, calling for Lucas.

Abby followed, echoing his shouts half-heartedly. The footprints soon faded under a stream of rainwater, and Abby started to suggest they turn back. Paxton looked like he was about to argue, but stopped as the walkie-talkie crackled to life.

Abby jolted in surprise, weeds tickling her knees. She held her breath and peered through the binoculars. Sure enough, Cassandra hovered ahead of Paxton, taking a slow step toward him, moving seamlessly through the brush. She circled him slowly, appraisingly, as her voice crackled soothingly through the walkie-talkie. "Paxton."

"Lucas!" Paxton called triumphantly, reaching for the walkie-talkie.

"That's not Lucas," Abby said gently. "You might want to sit down for this."

By the time wrinkles of confusion appeared on his brow, Cassandra was already speaking urgently. "It's me. Cassandra. Give him the binoculars, let him see for himself."

Abby removed the strap from around her neck and held the binoculars toward Paxton, who took a nervous step back. "I don't know—"

"Don't be such a worrywart," Cassandra said in a pushy yet friendly tone that reminded Abby of the way she often spoke to Lucas. "Isn't that what you always told me? Take the binoculars and *look*."

With a gulp, Paxton rested the crutches against a nearby tree and took the binoculars in his trembling hands. He raised them slowly, stopping before they met his pale blue eyes, and looked to Abby for instructions. Or reassurance.

"Be careful," she said. "Don't let them get wet."

Paxton let out a sharp breath and stepped back under the shelter of a large tree. Tightening his grip on the binoculars, he raised them. "Cass?"

"The one and only," Cassandra declared as lightning flashed in the distance. Without the binoculars, Abby could no longer see her, but she could picture her grinning at the reunion.

"I don't…I don't understand." Paxton lowered the binoculars and turned to Abby. "Where is she?"

"She's dead," Abby explained, an odd mixture of pity and jealousy knotting her stomach as his face fell. She remembered what it was like to lose hope, to know that someone you loved was dead, and she yearned for the chance to talk to Chelsea's spirit. "She's a ghost. And she needs our help."

Thunder grumbled as Paxton returned the binoculars to his eyes, seemingly addressing his question to Cassandra. "You—you're dead?"

"Yes," Cassandra said mournfully. "I was murdered."

"Oh my god." Paxton's face paled. His hands trembled around the binoculars and his voice squeaked. "Are you sure?"

"Yes, I'm pretty damn sure." Cassandra's voice crackled through the walkie-talkie at Abby's hip. "The problem is, I don't know who did it. That night, I followed Elena into the woods. Someone hit me on the back of the head."

"But…but you ran away," Paxton said wistfully. "They found your canoe."

"It wasn't mine."

Paxton leaned against the tree's gnarly trunk as if to steady himself, shock and understanding playing across his face. "Oh my god, Cass, I'm so sorry."

Abby imagined how dreadful it must be to find out someone died this way. She took a few steps back, wanting to give him space and time to process, but the storm was drawing closer. She wasn't sure how long they had before the worst of it hit.

"It's not your fault," Cassandra assured him. "But I need your help. I need to know who killed me."

Paxton let out a shaky breath as tears streamed down his face. He gave a series of increasingly faster nods. "Okay. I'll ask around, see what I can find out."

"Thank you." Cass's voice filled with gratitude. "You're still the best friend I could ever ask for."

Thunder roared, accentuating her words.

"You too." Paxton lowered the binoculars, wiped his eyes, and took a deep, shuddering breath. He turned to Abby. "Could you give us a moment?"

Abby hesitated, before cautiously handing over the walkie-talkie. "I'll be back in five minutes."

She moved toward the path until she was out of earshot, but close enough she could keep an eye on

Paxton in case he decided to run or did something incriminating, but he appeared to be intently listening, nodding along to a conversation that was drowned in the storm.

Abby longed to have such a reunion with Chelsea. Even if it was only just a few minutes. She wanted to tell her how sorry she was for inviting her to that stupid movie and how much she missed her and loved her to this day—and, maybe it was selfish, but she wanted Chelsea to see how far she'd come. To see Abby thriving, running her own business, helping people.

Chelsea would be proud. Right? *Chelsea's not perfect.* She ran her hands through her hair, trying to get Lucas's nagging voice out of her mind. She *was* perfect—she had to be—in all Abby's memories, she was carefree and joyful, compassionate and kind. She was Abby's perfect girlfriend, who had died tragically young.

Why couldn't Lucas just accept that?

By the time Paxton joined Abby, Abby's face was wet with a mix of rain and tears. He returned the binoculars and walkie-talkie in silence, his eyes puffy and red. He shoved his hands into his pockets, threw back his head, and let out a deep breath. "Come on. We still need to find Lucas."

"About that…" Abby took the binoculars back and peered through them long enough to see Cassandra giving her a thumbs-up. Her plan had worked. It was time to come clean.

Chapter Twelve

Abby spent the rest of Saturday giving Paxton his space and catching up on some much-needed romantic time with Mina. After dinner, they sipped hot chocolate and stayed up late, basking in the glow of Mina's string lights as they traded stories about their childhood and shared dreams of their futures. She woke to sunlight drifting through Mina's bedroom windows, illuminating the distant outline of the Blue Ridge Mountains in gorgeous pastel light.

Abby slipped out from under Mina's arm and tiptoed toward the window to get a better look. Mina was right. The view of the sparkling lake and dew-stained grasses rolling toward distant mountains was arguably even better than the pavilion's 360 view, although she could see only a few of the cabins.

They looked peaceful, with their dewy rooftops and empty porches. One of the campers slipped out of cabin one and headed toward the bathrooms, a bucket of shower supplies on his arm. Abby moved to the other window, and opened the blinds. Mina grunted in her sleep, rolling onto her stomach, where she promptly returned to snoring.

Abby's stomach growled. They must have food somewhere in this place. Not wanting to wake Mina, she quietly took a hoodie that had been draped over the chair and pulled it over her T-shirt. It smelled like Mina—beachy and nutty and soothing. She crept out into the hall, shutting the door quietly behind her. The cold hardwood floors chilled her bare feet, but she continued forward, hurrying downstairs.

Tantalizing scents of coffee and donuts wafted from downstairs, growing stronger as Abby neared the ground floor.

She headed toward the source—the kitchen.

Various creamers and sugars lined the counter, a fresh pot of coffee brewed at the far end. A large box of donuts lay open by the sink, their glazed surfaces melting in the morning sun.

Paxton sat at a long wooden table, a steaming mug and an empty plate in front of him. He glanced up as she entered.

Abby took in the dark bags under his eyes, his messy hair, and wrinkled T-shirt. He did not look like someone who had gotten a good night's sleep. But then again, who would sleep well after learning someone close to them was murdered? She felt a fresh wave of guilt at springing this on him. "Sorry about yesterday."

He shook his head, gesturing to the seat across from him. "I'm glad you let me talk to her."

Abby poured herself a mug of coffee—two creams, four sugars—placed a donut on a ceramic plate, and joined him.

He let out a shaky breath, running his thumb along the lip of the mug. "I still can't believe it. All this time, Elena was right."

"Right about what?"

"She kept telling me things didn't add up. She didn't think Cass would have taken a canoe out at night, much less run away."

Abby chewed her lip. Maybe Elena had seen more than she had let on. "Do you think she saw Cassandra following her that night?"

Paxton shook his head. "I don't think so—she didn't say anything about going out. Just that she and Cass had had an argument the day before, and Elena had gone to bed furious with her. Only to wake up and find out she'd gone missing."

"Why would she lie?" Abby asked, recalling how Elena had avoided answering her question.

Paxton shrugged. "I keep asking myself that. If she knew something more about what could have led to Cass's death, she would have told someone."

"Unless she thinks it incriminates her."

Paxton shook his head. "More like she thinks it's irrelevant. If she was involved—which, for the record, I can't imagine she would have been—then wouldn't she have wanted to corroborate the story that Cass had disappeared? Elena's spent years insisting that it wasn't an accident, and that Nick had something to do with it."

"Nick?" Abby asked, surprised.

Paxton leaned back with a sigh. He took a long sip of his coffee and chewed his lower lip, looking thoughtful. "He wasn't really over Cass. He could be pushy—not *horribly* pushy, but definitely persistent. He sent her flowers a few times, asked her to homecoming, left notes in her locker—Cass couldn't decide if she liked it or not. But Elena was protective of Cass and found his behavior infuriating."

Abby attempted to process this new information. Overly ambitious ex-boyfriend and overprotective sister were bound to clash. "Did Cassandra tell Nick to stop?"

"Not that I know of. The thing about Cass is that she wasn't really interested in dating anyone. She liked the idea of it. She liked Nick. But I don't think she was ever attracted to Nick."

"She was asexual?"

Paxton shrugged. "She was figuring things out. I think she was looking for some larger-than-life romanticized feeling of love, you know? Like what you see on TV. And when she didn't feel that with Nick, she wasn't sure what that meant."

Abby couldn't help but think about her feelings with Mina. For years, she had been missing that overwhelming swell of joy she felt when she had been with Chelsea. She had thought she'd never feel that way again. And it wasn't the same with Mina, not exactly. The joy was softer but more persistent. Something comforting rather than breathtaking. Could that also be love? Her insides twisted at the thought that love had somehow crept up on her without her realizing it.

"I don't think she ever shared those thoughts with Elena," Paxton continued. Abby forced herself to postpone examining her feelings for Mina in order to focus on his words, but her heart swelled at the thought that it was so close to love again. "Elena just saw her sister's ex sticking around like a creep. She was protective, even though she was younger. I think it was hard for her when Cass became a counselor, and she was still a camper. Two years can make a huge difference when you're sixteen and eighteen."

"Can you think of anyone else who would want to hurt Cass?"

"No," Paxton said. "And I can't even imagine Nick doing something like that. He was really shaken up over her disappearance. He drove around looking for her for days, kept calling her phone even though it went straight to voicemail. Cass liked him and trusted him, I just don't think she felt romantic toward him—or anyone—and that made her feel guilty."

"Do you think there's *any* chance Nick could have hurt Cass?"

Paxton rubbed his hand over his mouth. "God, I hope not. I want to say no…"

"But…?" Abby prompted.

"But I can't believe anyone would do such a thing. And someone clearly did. Cass didn't have enemies. Sure, she was a stickler for the rules. The campers were annoyed with her for enforcing bedtime or calling their parents when she found them making out in the woods. But it's not like anyone would kill her for that."

A bird soared past the window, fleeing before

several campers jogged past, accompanied by Jason and Heather, who took turns shouting words of encouragement. Abby was glad morning runs hadn't been one of the responsibilities she had been tasked with.

Paxton's gaze drifted toward the window and he took a sharp breath. "I just remembered something."

Abby leaned forward, intrigued. "What?"

Paxton shook his head as if he didn't want to say. His thumb traced the outline of mountains painted on his mug. He said softly, "The weekend before Cass went missing, she'd been talking to the police. They thought some of us were sneaking out to graffiti the town."

Abby remembered what Cassandra had said about the Brazen Brushstrokes and Elena's involvement. She wasn't sure if Paxton was aware that Elena had been involved or not. If Cassandra hadn't told him, she thought it best to refrain from sharing unless it became relevant.

"Some of the counselors and I—we were hanging out in the woods. Drinking. I know, it was stupid. We were young. It was like my third time drinking alcohol. Anyway, Cassandra led the police right to us. We saw them coming and ran. No one got caught, but they really cracked down on drinking after that. Mom said anyone found with alcohol in their possession would be fired immediately."

Abby was surprised she hadn't come across any of this information in Carol's files, but she supposed they hadn't connected the two events. "And you think someone could have killed Cassandra over that?"

Paxton's broad shoulders slumped in acknowledgment that it was a weak theory.

"We need Elena to open up about where she was going that night," Abby concluded. "She might not think it was important or had anything to do with Cassandra's death, but it could be the key to piecing this all together."

Paxton's T-shirt rustled as he leaned back in his chair and took a long sip from his mug. He sighed. "I'll talk to her. Any tips on how to broach the ghost subject?"

"I've found showing is better than telling."

Paxton shook his head. "Elena's too much of a skeptic. And she hates surprises. I'll talk to her. If I can convince her, I'll direct her to you."

"Good luck."

"Thanks." Paxton drained the rest of his mug. "I'm going to need it."

Chapter Thirteen

Abby lingered in the kitchen long after she'd finished breakfast and Paxton had retreated upstairs. She drummed her fingers along her empty mug and stared out the window as she considered what to do next. Paxton and Cassandra may be certain of Elena's innocence, but she was still the last person Cassandra remembered seeing. And she *had* lied to Paxton about being out that night. She was becoming more and more suspicious by the minute.

"Morning, sunshine." Mina's coffee-scented breath warmed her neck as strong arms wrapped around her shoulders. She planted a kiss on Abby's cheek.

Abby turned to her in surprise. "How long have you been down here?"

"Long enough to appreciate your thinking face." Mina returned to the counter where she picked up her mug and topped it off with more coffee. Abby noticed the warm, pleasant feelings Mina's presence stirred were back. That was a crush, sure. Intense passion. Close admiration. But love? "Any updates?"

Abby tensed, wondering how Mina could have read her thoughts, before she realized that Mina wasn't referring to the depth of their relationship and rather to the investigation. Abby sighed in relief. "Not much. Paxton is going to talk to Elena. See if she remembers anything that can help."

"That's great." Mina slipped into the chair beside Abby. "Does that mean you can take the rest of the day off?"

"I have to be back at three so Elena can take the afternoon off. Until then, I'm all yours."

"Perfect." Mina leaned forward, catching Abby's lips in a tender kiss that made Abby's heart flutter. She felt the word 'love' swirling in her mind, tugging at her feelings, prying them open as if they were a fortune cookie and the answer would be written on the inside. "The forecast says sunny all day. I'm going to finish my coffee, shower, and then maybe we can retry our picnic?"

"I love—" Abby started, and abruptly stopped herself. She shouldn't say it unless she was certain. Lucas had once told a girl he loved her on the third date and she never spoke to him again. Granted, they were way past the third date, but some people freaked out about these things. "—that idea," Abby concluded, feeling a sense of relief followed by immediate disappointment. She wished she could talk through her feelings with Mina, but asking someone she might be in love with to help her figure out whether or not her feelings were strong enough to be considered love would be hurtful, if not cruel. This was something she needed to figure out on her own.

WHEN ABBY finally found herself alone, she returned to her cabin to drop off her things. Having washed at Mina's the previous evening, she had no desire to plunge herself into the lukewarm water of the nearest showers and instead made her way toward the pavilion in search of Lucas.

She found him seated at a picnic table in the art pavilion, drawing in his sketchbook.

"How did it go with Paxton?" Lucas asked, glancing at Abby before finishing the shading on a superhero sketch. He then shut his sketchbook to give her his full attention.

"He and Cass had their reunion." Abby took a seat on the opposite side of the table and tried to act as if she wasn't still upset about his comment about Chelsea as she filled him in on all that had transpired in the past twenty-four hours.

When she finished, he shook his head. "I can't see Elena having anything to do with that."

"And you know her so well?" Abby winced as her words came out in an accusatory tone.

Lucas shrugged. "She's been helping me track down my art thief."

Abby groaned. "Will you let that go? It's just a bit of paint."

"It's not just one bottle. A bottle—or two—goes missing every class. Someone is messing with me, thinking I won't notice. But man, I noticed."

"Maybe they're borrowing it," Abby speculated.

"They haven't returned a single bottle."

"Not to you." A thought struck her. "But maybe they made their way to lost and found."

She jumped to her feet, glancing around the clearing for someone with a key to the boat shed. It was oddly empty now that most of the campers were at the optional Sunday retreat, and the rest were doing activities with their cabin counselors. Sabrina sat barefoot by the lake, her pink toenails glistening in the sand, a gardening hat blocking the sun as she read from a book in her lap.

"Sabrina," Abby shouted triumphantly, running toward her. "You have a key to the shed, right?"

"Why? Is something wrong?" Sabrina squinted up at Abby, adding a hand to the brim of her hat to better shield her eyes from the midday sun. She had a small splinter in her right hand and a faint marble-like scar across her forearm. Abby remembered that she had been in a cast the summer Cassandra went missing. Maybe Abby could find a way to use that as a segue into talking about that summer.

"Lucas is missing some art supplies," Abby said, realizing that she might also have a way in to questioning Sabrina about her dating life.

Sabrina blinked up at her curiously. "He thinks he left them in the shed?"

"He wants to check lost and found," Abby

explained, before adding quickly, "I hope you don't mind, but I overheard some of the others saying you were in a bad car accident a few years ago. Are you okay?"

"Oh, yeah." She shifted her toes in the sand, cracking the spine of her book until the cover was at the back and the current page she was reading was kept in the front. Abby hoped that wouldn't be a deal breaker for Lucas. He was pretty particular about the way people treated their books. "That was, like, ten years ago. It's all good."

"I crashed my car once," Abby said. It wasn't an outright lie, but more of an exaggeration—hitting the mailbox *had* left a nasty scratch on the front bumper. "My mom was so upset, she took my phone away for a week."

When Sabrina responded with a blank look, Abby continued. "I bet that was a rough summer for you. Hey, wasn't that the same summer the counselor went missing?"

Sabrina sighed. "It was a tough summer. My father is— frankly, he's an asshole. But I paid him back for the car and I got my own job and my own life and I cut him off, and I don't regret it. I'm doing pretty good for myself."

Abby thought of Sabrina's plain Jeep and wondered if the reason she didn't personalize it was because she was afraid of breaking it.

"Living that great single life," Lucas said. "Or maybe not single…?"

Abby could feel the tension rising off him in the

silence that followed, broken only by the lake's gentle waves. She flashed him an annoyed glance, but his attention was solely on Sabrina.

"Living that great single life," Sabrina confirmed. Abby couldn't tell if her smile was genuine, but she did pick up on the urgency in which Sabrina wanted to conclude the conversation as she shimmied her feet into her wedge shoes and stood. "I should get back to check on my campers."

Abby waited for Lucas to ask her out, but it seemed he had used up his boldness for the day. He stared at her book like a lost puppy. If he was going to hijack her investigation for his dating life, he could at least have the nerve to follow through with it.

"I still need a key to check lost and found," Abby said, pointing at the boating shed.

Sabrina wrinkled her nose. "Lost and found is in the Lodge. When you walk in, it's in the closet to your right."

"Well then what's that box of stuff I saw in the shed the other day?" Abby asked in confusion.

"Boating supplies?" Sabrina speculated.

"No, there were watches and jewelry and all sorts of odd stuff."

Sabrina's eyes widened. She stopped, retraced her steps until she was face to face with Abby. She glanced over her shoulder, and whispered, "Don't let the guys hear you talk about that."

That sure sounded suspicious. Lucas's concerned glance was probably meant to warn Abby to leave it alone, but she was curious, so she pressed. "What guys?"

"The guys—" Sabrina gestured to the lake, where several canoes raced down the river. Sun danced off Jason's blond locks and Nick's bare chest. Someone hollered as Nick's canoe reached the beach and he leaped out, holding his paddle over his head in triumph. Two boys jumped out of his canoe, copying him.

Sabrina stiffened. "Seriously, don't tell anyone else you know about that."

"About a box of stuff?" Abby asked, trying to figure out why some random objects would be so concerning. "Are they stealing?"

"Gambling?" Lucas asked at the same time.

Sabrina shook her head, took a small step back, and smiled. It was an odd, forced smile that didn't mask the fear in her eyes. "Sometimes things wash up on the beach. The guys find them, clean them up, and—if they don't belong to anyone here—*repurpose* them."

"Oh cool," Abby said, thinking of recycled art exhibits she had seen at local art shows back home. She had always wanted to get into art, and making abstract sculptures of lost items seemed easy enough, but the one time she had tried to build a castle out of bottle caps, she had gotten bored building the front gates and then her mother threw it out thinking it was trash.

"Not cool," Lucas countered. "She means they sell them."

Sabrina winced, confirming Lucas's suspicion. She gripped Abby's arm and pleaded, "Please, don't mention it to anyone. Nick's brother's sick. He's been using the extra cash to help cover his medical bills."

"Do you trust him?" Abby asked.

Sabrina hesitated. "Nick? He's a good guy."

"But do you trust him?"

Sabrina tucked a strand of hair behind her ear and shrugged, her gaze flickering to Lucas and back. "I guess. I've got to go. Good luck with your paint."

She turned and walked briskly toward her cabin, leaving her towel in the sand.

Lucas shook his head in disapproval, but Abby knew him well enough to know he wasn't going to do anything about it—except perhaps glare in Nick's direction now and again. "He better not be selling my paint."

"That would be the world's worst business model," Abby replied. "Come on, let's check lost and found."

Lucas's paint was not in the lost and found closet. There was, however, a very fancy writing pen that made Lucas reconsider, for several minutes, his stance on claiming other people's lost items. Ultimately, it was decided that he would stand by his principles and leave the pen for the rightful owner to claim—at least, for now.

Abby joined Mina in the kitchen, packed supplies for their picnic, and headed past the dining room, where Lucas was half reading and half eyeing the lost and found closet.

The outdoors greeted them with a refreshing breeze. Abby and Mina meandered back to the clearing in the woods, enjoying each other's company as much as the golden sunshine that enveloped them. This time, they finished their meal without interruption. They snuggled side by side, hands intertwined, watching thin white clouds drift past.

"I've been thinking about Cassandra," Mina said.

Abby turned toward her with curiosity. She had been making an effort *not* to bring up Cassandra during their alone time.

"Everyone says she was a stickler for the rules. That's how I was at her age."

"I'm glad you've lightened up." Abby playfully brushed her shoulder against Mina's, stirring that warm, pleasant feeling in her core.

Mina's lips tilted toward a smile but tightened into a grimace. She picked up a dandelion and twisted the stem between her fingers. "I wasn't just a stickler for the rules. I was kind of a jerk about it."

Abby had a difficult time imagining Mina, with her carefree attitude, had been a jerk about the rules. "How so?"

"I got so many people in trouble for copying each other's homework. Even if it was as simple as a word search. And don't get me started on what happened at swim practice."

"You were on the swim team?"

"Until senior year. I thought about swimming competitively for college, but Mom was sick and— let's just say I gave up on caring about the rules so much when it felt like the universe stopped following its own rules."

Abby squeezed Mina's hand, knowing how much Mina missed her mom.

"I genuinely thought that rules were put in place to keep people safe. Stop at a red light and no one will get hurt. But apparently you can stop at every red light, never run a stop sign, and you'll still die young."

Abby leaned her head on Mina's shoulder. They both knew there were no words to ease the pain of losing a loved one. Wind danced through the clearing, sending hundreds of dandelion puffs soaring past their blanket. One landed on Mina's eyelash. Abby brushed it away with her thumb. Mina didn't even wince. There was something special in the way she relaxed around Abby, so soft and trusting. It was a sharp contrast to the guarded way she had been when they first met.

"Anyway," Mina continued, "I was trying to say that I understand Cassandra. If she saw someone breaking the rules, she would have turned them in—no questions, no justifications, no excuses. What if she saw someone doing something wrong, but she didn't realize what she had seen?"

"What do you mean?" Abby asked, trying to picture how that would work. "She couldn't turn someone in if she didn't realize they were breaking the rules."

"Right, but what if the murderer *thought* she was going to turn them in?"

Abby frowned. "You think someone killed her to

keep her from telling on them? Isn't murder a lot worse of a crime than drinking or making out in the woods?"

"You would think so, but if someone was drunk and scared—"

Abby shuddered at the thought. It was a solid theory. She imagined Cassandra about to crash a secret party, with startled counselors attempting to hide their tracks and running away…

"But it was storming," Abby pointed out, her visualization dissolving. "They wouldn't have been partying out here in a storm."

"Teenagers can be stupid," Mina said. "I know I've—"

Mina fell quiet as frantic footsteps headed toward them. A camper rushed past, her long blonde hair flapping against her white collared shirt as she headed toward camp.

Abby jumped to her feet and called, "Lilly?"

The girl glanced over her shoulder. Sure enough, it was Lilly, dressed in her church uniform of all white except for a red tie, and the Power Ranger sneakers that she had insisted on wearing. She turned and ran toward Abby.

"What's going on?" Abby asked, scanning for signs of any other campers. They usually traveled in packs, and were never supposed to go somewhere alone. "Where's your buddy?"

"What happened to your arm?" Mina asked with concern.

Lilly hid her hand protectively, but not before Abby noticed a thin pink scratch. Giving Mina a suspicious look, Lilly gestured for Abby to come closer.

Abby stepped forward and Lilly cupped her hands around her mouth, reaching up on her tiptoes. Abby crouched down to make it easier for her.

Lilly whispered, "Amy's trying to get the kitten."

"What kitten?"

Lilly shushed her, gave an exaggerated sigh, and said at normal volume, "Our kitten! He ran away!" She tugged on Abby's elbow. "Please, come help before it gets hurt."

Abby stood, shrugging in acceptance. Of all the campers' odd requests she had heard in recent weeks, this was far from the weirdest. "Lead the way."

Lilly resumed running back to the trail, her pigtails flapping.

"Go ahead," Mina suggested, reaching for the picnic basket. "I'll pack up and be there in a minute."

Abby smiled in appreciation. She wasn't sure what she had done to earn someone as thoughtful and practical as Mina, but it was probably her most rewarding accomplishment yet. That was if Mina didn't leave her.

"Hurry!" Lilly shouted.

Abby broke into a run, hoping the kitten wasn't too far away. Thankfully, she reached Lilly in less than a minute, and slowed as Lilly shoved a honeysuckle-wrapped shrub aside and disappeared off the path, into the woods. Abby kept an eye out for poisoned ivy as she followed, wishing she had paid better attention during orientation. Did it have five leaves or six? Either way, the ground was surprisingly easy to traverse. Even though it wasn't a clear path, it was flat like a deer trail, littered in leaves, pine needles, and debris. Since it was entirely hidden from the main path, she worried Mina would have a hard time finding them.

"How much further?" Abby asked, as the makeshift path opened into a large dirt path with layers of old tractor marks down the center.

"Just over there." Lilly pointed to a thicket of trees surrounding a wooden cabin with a stone chimney.

For a moment Abby feared they had left the campgrounds and were trespassing on someone's private property, but as the breeze parted the trees, revealing vine-ridden windows and rotting wood, it became clear this building had long been abandoned.

A patch of ferns parted and Amy stepped out, her clothes splattered with dirt, pink glasses slanted. She rushed toward Abby, pointing at the side of the house. "He's up there!"

Abby studied the building closer and noticed a black kitten sitting on the ledge of a second-story window. He was small—slightly bigger than Abby's palm—and basking in sunlight.

"He must be so scared," Lilly said, as the kitten licked his front paw.

Abby thought he looked rather pleased with himself, but she kept that to herself as she tapped the trunk of a nearby tree and called, "Here, kitty, kitty, kitty." If she could get him to jump to the branch, she could try to catch him.

The kitten was not interested. He didn't even pause his licking or glance in her direction.

"Do you have any food or treats?" Abby asked the girls.

They shook their heads.

"We gave all the bacon to the other kittens," Amy said sheepishly.

"There's more?" Of course there were. Abby scratched her head, torn between wanting to make the girls happy and having no idea what to do with a litter of kittens.

"They went inside," Lilly explained.

"There's a ladder," Amy offered.

"Inside there?" Abby pointed at the old building. "You've been inside?"

"No," Lilly said. "The door's locked."

That was a relief. Judging from the state of the outside, there was no telling what the inside was like. While she was all for exploring, she didn't want the girls to end up being sent home with tetanus.

"You can see it through the window," Lilly said brightly.

"Oh, the poor cat! He must be worried sick." Amy clenched the front of her shirt and began to cry. "Please rescue him, please."

The sight of Amy's large blue eyes welling with tears and the sound of her sniffles tugged on something inside Abby. She wondered if Amy knew she had that effect and was faking it. If she did, she was good.

"Okay, I'll see what I can do," Abby said, trying the nearest door. The handle was old and rusty. Metallic paint flaked against her palm. It hardly turned, and the door wouldn't budge.

She moved around to the front of the house and tried that door. Also locked.

"I told you it was locked," Lilly said.

Amy pointed to a brownish-green tarp covering the side of the building. "Try the window."

It seemed like a bad idea, but Abby couldn't help but peel back the tarp to see what was underneath. Foggy glass stood between her and a large room with stone flooring and a fireplace. It was much nicer than Abby had expected—as if it could have once been lived in. There were sconces on the walls, a ceiling fan, and even a set of built-in shelves. But it was nearly empty, with several pieces of mismatched furniture, a single folding chair, and a ladder.

Abby wriggled her fingers into a gap under the window and found it lifted easily. She slid it up wide enough that she could crawl inside.

"Hello?" she called. "Is anyone home?"

"No one's there," Lilly said, like she was worried about Abby's sanity. "It's falling apart."

"I just wanted to check," Abby said.

"There's the ladder." Amy pointed excitedly. "Hurry!"

Abby hoisted herself onto the window ledge and lowered herself inside. Her sneakers squeaked softly against the stone floor. For an abandoned building in the woods, this place was in pretty good condition. Sure, it wasn't livable, but 'falling apart' was a bit of an exaggeration. There was some mold and peeling damask wallpaper, but the structure itself appeared solid. As Abby approached the ladder, a red box caught her eye. She paused. It was cracked open, revealing a set of tools. The box was red—the same shape and size as the one she had seen both Nick and Jason with. Could Jason have been here that day she and Lucas had seen him coming out of the woods? Why would he be in an abandoned building?

She could think of several reasons, none of them good, as she proceeded with caution. The last thing she wanted to do was stumble across Cassandra's body in a closet. Or actually, the last thing she wanted to do was stumble across the person who *murdered* Cassandra, anywhere in this house.

As Abby started to move the ladder, another thought occurred to her—if the stairs were in as good condition as the rest of the house, she could go up to the second floor and open the window to rescue the cat without having to worry about scaring him away with a giant ladder.

Lilly and Amy watched her from the window, gesturing for her to hurry.

"I'll be right back," Abby said, moving deeper into the house. "Stay there!"

"But the ladder!" Amy grabbed the roots of her hair as if she was in great distress.

"Stay there," Abby repeated, trying her best to sound authoritative as she started up the L-shaped stone staircase that spanned a wide entryway between the previous living room and what must have once been a kitchen. There was no railing, but the stairs were intact. Still, Abby pressed her hand against the peeling wall as she ascended cautiously.

At the top, she reached a narrow hall with a door to her left and three empty doorways to her right: one on each side of the hall and one at the far end. The cat had been on the back window, so he should be outside the room on her left.

The brass knob chilled her hand as she turned it. The door clicked open, hinges creaking as she pressed it open. Sure enough, the window across from her was lined with a tiny black cat.

Abby tiptoed cautiously into the room, not wanting to scare the cat, which was clearly enjoying basking in the sunlight. She wished she had brought something to carry the cat in, or at least prevent it from scratching her. She glanced around the room. It was nearly empty, except for a fancy fireplace, moth-eaten curtains, and a lopsided antique wooden dresser.

In front of the fireplace, a red blanket lay curled in a circle beside a small bowl of water and an empty plastic bowl that Abby suspected had been licked clean of cat food. Abby picked up the blanket and found it in surprisingly good condition, except for a few cat hairs. It looked far newer than anything else in the house—except perhaps the toolbox. And familiar. Examining it closer, she found the Camp Pine Whispers logo embroidered in the corner.

She shuddered, and looked at the tag for any signs that the blanket belonged to Jason. There weren't any, of course. The only thing she found, other than cat hair and dirt, was a faint drop of pastel-pink paint.

While she didn't think of Jason as a painter, it was possible he—or one of his campers—had painted at some point this summer. She moved cautiously to the windowsill, trying to focus on the kitten that continued to bathe itself, oblivious to her presence. Her brief time working at a cat cafe had taught her the basics of handling foster cats, but strays were another matter entirely. She wasn't sure if this cat would let her touch him, much less pick him up. Abby opened the window slowly, hoping she wouldn't startle the cat into falling.

The kitten craned his neck, green eyes peering curiously from an adorable face covered in black fur. Abby held her hand out for him to sniff. His nose wrinkled. He stood, arching his spine, and rubbed his chin against Abby's fingers.

That was a surprisingly positive start. Abby scratched his tiny chin with one finger and he replied with a resounding purr. It didn't take much effort to scoop him up. "I know some kids who are going to be very happy to see you."

The kitten settled into her arms, rubbing his face against the fleece blanket as Abby started down the stairs. Sun streamed through the open window, shining off the ornate trim. What was this place? It was far too fancy to have been a cabin, but there were no roads connected to it. If it were any bigger, she would have thought it was some luxury mountain hotel that had gone out of business, but there were so few rooms upstairs. In the corner of her vision, a single red light winked. Abby turned, scanning the empty walls for the source. Tucked into the far corner of the entryway, a small camera hung from the ceiling, its lens pointed toward the front door, a red light blinking over it.

Someone was watching this place. Someone was watching *her*.

Abby hurried the rest of the way outside, scrambling through the open window to Lilly's and Amy's cheers and applause, the kitten tucked safely in her arms. As they headed back toward camp, she couldn't help but glance over her shoulder, wondering why someone would leave a camera in an abandoned building—and more importantly, if they had caught her breaking and entering.

Chapter Fourteen

"I'm not sure this is a good idea." Mina frowned in the direction of Lilly and Amy, who were sitting cross-legged by the foot of her bed, peering into a box of kittens.

"It'll just be for a few days," Abby assured her. She stretched, massaging the ache in her shoulder that had developed while she gathered the rest of the kittens with some canned tuna she had found in the kitchen and a box from the dumpster. "I'll drop them off at the humane society on my next day off."

Mina gave her a doubtful look.

"Come on," Abby encouraged, "They're so cute!"

Nibbles, as Lilly had affectionately named the black kitten, lay snuggled between his siblings. It had taken some gentle prying before Lilly admitted that she had been sneaking food to the kittens the past few days, but she knew nothing about the blanket or the food and water bowls. They had seen no signs of an adult cat, and the kittens had been friendly enough from the start —someone had been taking care of them. But surely no one lived in that place?

With all the time she'd spent looking into Cassandra's murder, she had become a terrible counselor. She'd have to make more of an effort to keep an eye on her campers.

"They are cute," Mina admitted, kneeling beside Lilly and affectionately stroking the nearest gray kitten. She twitched in her sleep before purring at Mina's strokes. "Fine. But just one week."

Abby grinned. "And you thought you were a stickler for the rules."

"How times have changed," Mina said fondly, returning to Abby's side. She whispered, "But for the record, Nibbles is a terrible name."

"Don't let Lilly hear you say that," Abby whispered back. Lilly was busy adjusting the pillowcase around the edge of the box. Lilly had wanted to use the blanket Abby had found, but Mina had insisted they wash it first, and offered a pillowcase as a temporary alternative.

Abby chewed her nails as she thought about the blanket rolling around in the wash and the camera that had watched her steal it.

"What are you thinking?" Mina asked, moving toward the head of her bed, as far from the kids as the room allowed.

Abby slipped her fingers into her pockets as she

joined Mina at her headboard. A breeze drifted through the open window, ruffling the pictures hanging from a string behind Mina's bed. Many were several years old—a number featured Mina as a teenager with someone who could only be her mom: Mina and her mom in blue aprons, holding a tray of gorgeously decorated cookies; Mina in a prom dress, with her mom kissing her cheek; Mina between both parents in her high-school graduation cap and gown. There were a few recent photos with friends Abby didn't recognize, and a few of Michelle's wedding, where Mina and Abby had first met. Of the two dozen photos, there was only one of Abby—a single selfie of her and Mina grinning from a secret passageway they had found over Valentine's Day. The lighting on the photo was terrible, but Abby felt a sense of pride at having a space on Mina's wall, while simultaneously craving more.

"Don't tell me you're second-guessing the kittens," Mina whispered in all seriousness.

Abby shook her head, realizing her thoughts had wandered. "It's not the kittens. It's that place."

On the walk back from the woods, she had filled Mina in on where she had found the kitten. She had skimmed over the part about the camera, but it troubled her more with each passing moment. "There was a camera. Someone saw me go in there."

"You rescued a cat," Mina countered. "From an abandoned house. The camera probably hasn't been turned on in years."

"Maybe," Abby admitted. "It was…strange. Half

abandoned, maybe. Like someone had started moving out, and stopped before they'd finished."

"Sounds like it's being used for storage."

It didn't look like any storage unit she had seen. Then again, most of her experience in storage units came from TV.

"You could ask Paxton about it," Mina continued. "It's camp property, right? I'm pretty sure he would know."

"I guess so," Abby said, unable to keep the knots in her shoulders from tightening as she thought of the paint stain on the blanket. Maybe she was overthinking this. Maybe it really was an old building turned into storage and Paxton had simply put up a camera to keep an eye on the kittens. "Is Paxton an artist?"

Mina shrugged. "Not that I know of."

Abby suddenly thought of Lucas's missing paint and massaged her forehead. Maybe she should have paid more attention to him. Perhaps the missing paint and the creepy house were connected.

"You, the kids, and the kittens are all home safe," Mina replied, placing a warm hand on Abby's shoulder. "That's the most important thing."

Abby gave her an appreciative smile as she relaxed under her touch. Outside, the clock chimed, signaling it was time for dinner.

Abby groaned. "I'm going to be in so much trouble for being late."

"You found two lost campers and escorted them to the nurse's office," Mina countered with a devious smile. "I think you'll find yourself rewarded for that behavior."

"Is that so?"

Abby leaned forward, meeting Mina in a kiss that sent all thoughts of the camera from her mind.

Chapter Fifteen

"How do you manage to get into this much trouble?" Lucas asked at breakfast the next morning. His stubble was longer than Abby had seen it before, forming a hint of a beard. Paired with his gold wire-framed glasses, it gave him a sophisticated look.

"It's not like I got caught." Abby took a bite of her pancake, pleased with her summary of yesterday's events.

"Unless someone saw you on camera," Lucas countered.

Abby waved her hand dismissively. After a good night's rest, her fear of the camera had all but dissipated. "Like Carol is going to kick me out for rescuing a cat."

"How far exactly was this house from your picnic?"

"Not far. It's just really overgrown and easy to miss."

Lucas leaned across the table toward her, so he

could lower his voice and still be heard over the campers' morning chatter. "Didn't you have your picnic in the same place we saw Cassandra's ghost?"

"Yeah. So?"

Lucas set down his fork and looked pointedly at Abby. "So…that place may be abandoned now, but who knows if it was ten years ago."

Abby felt her eyes widen. "You think someone was there the night Cassandra died?"

Lucas glanced toward the woods, the pinkening sunrise reflected in his glasses. "Could be where the killer was hiding."

"The killer could be caught on camera," Abby added, jumping to her feet. "We've got to ask Paxton —"

Lucas grabbed Abby's elbow, jerking her back into her seat. "Uh, no, we've got to think about this. If there *was* something on that camera, that means someone saw it. Most likely that *someone* was Paxton's mom."

"So we can ask her, then," Abby said excitedly.

"Bad idea," Lucas stressed. "If she saw something, then she hid it from everyone—including the police. Which means she knows who killed Cassandra and she's protecting them. Who do you think she's most likely to protect?"

"Paxton," Abby said with a sinking feeling.

"Yeah," Lucas said somberly.

"But we don't know that the camera was even there back then," Abby added. "Or that the killer had anything to do with the house."

"True. But why isn't that building on any of the maps?"

Abby snapped her fingers. "The memory book. The one from the library has an old map that we can check against the current one. If that building *was* on the map back then, and it isn't now, you could be onto something."

"What are we whispering about?" a third voice whispered.

Abby jumped. Elena was kneeling behind her and Lucas, her brown eyes waiting expectantly for an answer.

"Campus maps," Abby said, wondering how much she had heard.

"I've got one in my bunk," Elena supplied, her voice as flat as ever. "If you want to borrow it, feel free."

"Thanks," Abby said. "But I've got one in my bunk too."

"What do you need?" Elena asked, tapping her forehead. "I've got a photographic memory. I can guide you pretty much anywhere."

"Do you know of any abandoned buildings in the woods?" Abby studied her response.

Elena tilted her head in thought, her forehead wrinkling. "I haven't come across any. Is it on camp property?"

"Yeah," Abby said. "At least, I think so. What else is around here?"

Elena shrugged. "State park borders on the west. Some private land on the east. And who knows about the land to the north—it's mostly wilderness prone to landslides."

Behind Elena, Hannah giggled as Jason planted a kiss on her cheek. Abby noticed that she was wearing a shark-tooth necklace that looked suspiciously like Jason's, which was absent from its usual place around his neck. Sabrina watched them, blushing behind her pancakes as she darted a glance at Abby—no, at Lucas. Had he finally gotten the courage to ask her out?

She turned to Lucas to see how he'd respond, but he didn't seem to notice. His attention was still on Elena as he said, "I thought Paxton's family owned this whole mountain, even past the campgrounds."

"They own most of it," Elena agreed. "A lot more than the campgrounds. But they sold some of it a few years back."

Jason laughed loudly at something Hannah said and as Abby's attention turned toward him, she couldn't help but feel like he was the one who had brought the toolbox into the abandoned building. But why? Paxton mentioned Jason had been drinking in the woods the night Cassandra had called the police. Jason could have been drinking that night in the storm, tucked safely in that old building. That might have even been where he stored all his alcohol. She imagined him seeing Cassandra in a flash of lightning, panicking, and turning to violence. Maybe the alcohol was still there, hidden under the floorboards.

Lucas asked, "Do you remember exactly how many years ago?"

"A year after Cassandra died," Elena said blankly.

"Speaking of which, Paxton says you've found her ghost. I want to talk to her."

Abby stared at her in stunned silence. This was what she had been waiting for, but she hadn't expected Elena to accept it so easily. She searched Lucas's expression for some clue as to whether or not he thought this was a good idea, but all she saw was surprise.

"I'll need to be there with you," Abby said.

Elena nodded as she slipped her phone from her back pocket. "Friday, then. Eighty percent chance of rain that afternoon. The kids will come in for a movie. I'll let Paxton know we'll both slip out for an hour or two."

"Friday," Abby repeated, surprised by how soon that was. Only four days away. She had been hoping for at least a week to think this through. Elena was the last person Cassandra saw alive. This reunion could be the key to unlocking Cassandra's memory—or revealing that Elena is in fact a dangerous murderer. She would need to prepare for either outcome.

"It's settled, then," Elena said. "See you Friday."

ABBY SPENT the following days avoiding Elena as much as possible, which was unsurprisingly difficult considering they slept twelve feet apart and shared responsibility for the same campers. On Monday evening, she ensured she focused on the campers as much as possible—she read them stories, performed magic tricks, and braided hair until her fingers ached—anything to avoid having a private conversation with Elena. On Tuesday, she started a water balloon fight. On Wednesday, she got the kids to perform skits around the campfire until curfew. On Thursday, when the skies were gray and rain threatened to fall, she suggested they mix up the hiking groups under the pretense that the kids had a chance to interact with more kids outside their cabin.

"Great idea!" Jason's voice boomed through the forest. "Campers, line up. Counselors, find someone who isn't in your cabin to team up with."

Abby took a step away from Jason, still not entirely convinced he wasn't the one who had killed Cassandra.

Elena's dark eyes flashed, but she made no protest as she turned her back to Abby and moved into the crowd. Abby started toward Lucas, then noticed Nick moving toward Sabrina, who was glancing tentatively at Lucas.

Abby intercepted Nick. "Want to team up?"

Nick blinked, clearly surprised by her question. He scratched his beard and shrugged. "Sure. Why not?"

When Abby glanced at Lucas, she saw Sabrina at his side, her hand brushing his shoulder. She bit back a smile. Lucas owed her one.

The conversation was mostly occupied by the campers until they were a good length down the trail and it widened enough for two people to walk comfortably side by side. Nick ushered the kids to go ahead until only he and Abby were left.

"Shouldn't one of us be in the front?" Abby asked.

Elena had been insistent that a counselor must walk in front of the kids and another at the rear.

Nick adjusted his baseball cap. "They've walked this path a dozen times. It's not like they'll get lost. And we haven't gotten a chance to bond yet. I like to get to know all the new faces around here."

He said it like he owned the place, followed by an unspoken addition that he had sway over how long the new faces stuck around. If he wanted information from her, she would play along and get what she could from him as well. She plastered on a smile. "What do you want to know?"

"How are you finding camp life so far?"

Abby tried to hide her surprise at such an innocent question. She answered honestly. "It's fun, but a lot of work. I love being outdoors but I miss having internet access. And air conditioning."

Nick laughed. "My two biggest camp peeves, for sure. You get used to it after a while. At least this summer heat isn't too bad. Last year it was brutal."

Abby let the small talk continue for a while, trading shows they were most looking forward to watching when they got home, until he seemed at ease. When she felt it was time to press him, she said, as lightly as possible, "You know, you're not as bad as Elena made you out to be."

She had prepared for Nick to show signs of anger, but he merely let out a heavy sigh. "Elena and I have a complicated history."

"Oh?" Abby waited for him to explain as he continued forward, sun glistening off his plastic wristbands with motivational quotes. She recalled what Sabrina had said about Nick's brother being sick and wondered if the bracelets were for related charities. She also recalled that he had been selling items washed up on the beach. She wondered how long ago that started —if Cassandra had known about it and tried to put a stop to it.

When it became clear Nick wasn't going to offer more, Abby pressed, "Because of Cassandra?"

Nick turned back to her with a heavy look. "Yeah, because of Cass. Elena didn't like how we left things. She thinks I had something to do with Cass running away. I don't blame her. I wasn't really nice to Elena back then. Now I just want her to be okay. She has this obsession—you may have noticed—with what happened."

"You mean how she thinks Cassandra was murdered?"

Nick gave a long, slow nod, his beard brushing the collar of his polo. "She listens to all these true crime podcasts. Thinks someone kidnapped Cass and drowned her or something. I keep telling her things like that don't happen, and she turns it around on me. Says things like 'fifty-four percent of murders are caused by someone they knew' and 'domestic or former domestic partners are the most probable perpetrator.' It's exhausting. And if it's this exhausting for me, how much worse must it be for her? Spending all her time coming up with dead-end theories."

"What do you think happened to Cassandra?" Abby asked.

Nick removed his baseball cap and ran his hands through his thick, dark curls. "Maybe she did try to run. There was a bad storm that night. Maybe she got lost in the woods or caught in a landslide. I wish I knew why she went out that night. I wish I could have stopped her."

"You don't think there's a chance she's still alive?"

Nick's lips tightened as he rubbed his jaw. "If she was, she would have contacted Elena by now."

The breeze picked up, scattering debris. A cold raindrop landed on Abby's shoulder, sending goosebumps down her arm.

"Don't let her get to you," Nick said, in a tone that could have been comforting or a warning.

"Cassandra?" Abby whispered, wondering if he had heard about Cassandra's ghost.

"Elena," Nick clarified. "She can be a bit obsessed. What happened with Cassandra was a tragic accident. But it was years ago. She needs to move on, live her life. It's not good for her to keep coming back here, obsessing."

"You keep coming back here," Abby pointed out. "Paxton and the others do too."

"It's different. We come here because we have fond memories that we want to protect *despite* what happened with Cass. Elena hates it here. She always has. And yet, she keeps coming back, hoping she'll find some clue as to what happened that night. It's not healthy."

Abby thought of herself in the aftermath of Chelsea's death—replaying everything that had led up to her final moments, every text she had sent that day, every word of their last conversation. She wondered if Elena shared a similar guilt and was looking for a way to absolve it—for someone to blame other than herself. She nodded, acknowledging Nick's words, although she took away a very different meaning than he likely intended. Elena was desperate for answers. As much as Abby hated to admit it, she was probably their best bet at solving this case. "I'll keep that in mind."

"Good." Nick's face brightened. "We should probably catch up to the kids and head back to camp. It looks like it's about to rain. Wonder what movie we'll watch this time?"

A cold raindrop landed on Abby's nose. Leaves overhead trembled with intermittent rain splatter.

She had a promise to keep.

Chapter Sixteen

"If this is a prank, I'll kill you."

Elena's words were not the least bit comforting as Abby led her deeper into the woods. Rain drizzled against Abby's thin robin's-egg-blue rain jacket and splattered her sneakers. She squinted as she adjusted her hood for the dozenth time, only for it to promptly slip back down her damp hair. Elena was better prepared in a black raincoat and matching rain boots. Not a single strand of *her* hair was wet.

"It's not a prank," Abby insisted, turning up the volume on the walkie-talkie clipped to her jean shorts until she could hear the static. "But there's also no guarantee we'll see Cassandra."

"You're lucky I trust Paxton," Elena said. "Or I wouldn't be here."

Abby did not consider herself lucky to be out in the cold, rainy woods alone with Elena, but she kept that thought to herself as the world turned gray and foggy through the binoculars, with the landscape ever shifting.

"How much farther?" Elena asked.

Abby scanned the trees around the area where she had first met Cassandra, but there was no sign of her. She moved around the bend, ignoring Elena's heavy sigh, until she reached the rain-soaked clearing where Cassandra had interrupted her picnic with Mina. It was now mostly mud.

"Now, we wait." Abby lowered the binoculars, adjusted her hood, and turned back to Elena.

"Great." Elena raised her headphones to her ears. "Tell me if something interesting happens."

Under other circumstances, Abby would have found Elena's lack of social skills annoying at most, a challenge at best, but she preferred the silence to Elena's cold cynicism. Elena shifted her weight, leaning against the damp base of a tall tree.

"Cassandra?" Abby whispered, as if the name alone would be enough to summon the spirit.

Careful to avoid the worst of the mud, Abby slowly made her way around the edge of the clearing. Waves lashed the shore as the lake rose dangerously close to the trail. The rain increased, pounding her back. It was a good thing she had taken in the kittens—this storm was brutal.

Elena gasped in alarm. Abby turned to find her headphones on the ground, her feet dangling inches above the earth. A quick glance through the binoculars confirmed her fear—Cassandra's face twisted with desperation as she gripped Elena by the shoulders, pinning her to the tree.

Abby turned the walkie-talkie up, running to help Elena. "What are you doing? This is Elena!"

"I know." Cassandra's voice boomed through the walkie-talkie.

Abby stumbled, uncertain what to do. She hadn't anticipated Cassandra could be dangerous. She hadn't seemed that upset or hostile before. But if Elena had played a role in her death—

"Cass?" Elena squinted, trying to see the ghost with her own eyes.

"It's me." Cassandra sounded desperate, pleading. "You were the last person I saw, *Elena*. I need to know what happened."

Elena's eyes widened. Rain dripped down her face, but she made no effort to claw Cassandra's ghostly form away from her. She merely shook her head, her dark braids coming undone against the bark. "I… I don't know."

"What were you doing that night?" Cassandra's voice cut through the rain, growing in volume. "Who were you meeting?"

Abby wished she had thought to bring the salt gun. She didn't want to use it against Cassandra, but the clear urgency in her voice and the way she kept Elena pinned against the tree, bark digging into her rain jacket—she was teetering on the edge of dangerous.

Elena's eyebrows pinched together, her face growing pale. "I don't know what you're talking about."

"Don't lie to me." Cassandra tightened her grip on

Elena. Elena winced, biting her lower lip as she shook her head.

Abby wondered who she could possibly be protecting. She didn't seem close to anyone at camp—except perhaps Paxton, but Cassandra seemed to trust him most of all.

"I *saw* you." Cassandra's voice crackled. "You snuck out. I followed you, and I *died*."

Tears fell from Elena's eyes. She attempted to wipe them away, but Cassandra grabbed her hand, freezing her in place.

"I didn't," Elena insisted. "After we argued, I went back to my cabin. I was so upset, I cried for hours. I missed dinner. By the time I felt like getting up and taking a shower, it was too dark and the storm was bad. So I wrote you a letter. An apology. I'd planned on giving it to you the next day, but you were…"

"Dead?" Cassandra finished. She let go of Elena, who gasped as she tumbled to the ground. Elena scrambled to her knees, rubbing at her puffy red eyes.

Abby found herself longing to believe her. She seemed genuinely shaken.

Rain pounded through Cassandra as she paced back and forth in front of Elena. Wind pooled unnaturally at her feet, following her footsteps, sending twigs and leaves swirling around her waist like a skirt. This wasn't a good sign.

Abby passed Elena the binoculars, keeping her gaze on the swirling debris. "Try not to upset her."

"Cass," Elena pleaded, her voice cracking. "I've missed you so much—"

"Shut up!" Cassandra's voice reverberated through the trees. "I'm trying to think!"

This was escalating quickly. Abby suggested, "Why don't we leave you to your thoughts for a bit, and come back tomorrow—"

"No!" Elena and Cassandra both shouted at once. Elena sounded desperate, while Cassandra sounded cold and commanding. Abby twisted her salt necklace, contemplating her next move. She wanted to give them more time together, but not if Elena's life was in danger.

Elena reached toward the swirling dirt. "Cass, I had nothing to do with the night you died, I swear—"

"Don't touch me!" Cassandra snapped. Dirt, twigs, and pebbles shot out in every direction.

Abby covered her face as they pelted her rain jacket. When the assault stopped, she lowered her arms to see Elena doing the same.

"Okay, let's talk this through, then," Abby said diplomatically. "Cassandra, are you sure it was Elena that you followed?"

"Yes." Cassandra's voice boomed through the storm, then softened, stones clattering to the forest floor as the wind died down. "I mean—I don't remember. But it was you, Elena. It must have been. I was up waiting for you and you left—you moved past my cabin, head down, hood raised."

"That could have been anyone," Elena reasoned.

"It was *you*." A fresh swarm of plant matter rose from the ground, swirling in the growing wind as Cassandra's voice thundered. "I loved you,

Elena! You were my sister, and you led me to my death!"

"No! I—" Elena broke into a fit of coughing as Cassandra slammed them with another wave of debris.

Abby shielded her eyes, wincing as a piece of damp bark caught in the sleeve of her jacket, scraping her wrist. "We should go."

Elena shook her head, spitting out a mouthful of dirt. "Cass!"

A loud series of cracks echoed around the clearing. At first, Abby thought it was some odd form of thunder, but then she saw the branches surging toward Cass. Cass was gathering weapons.

"We've got to go, now," Abby insisted, reaching for the binoculars.

Elena tightened her grip, pulling the binoculars out of Abby's reach. "Not until she believes me!"

Spindly sticks charged toward them. Abby tackled Elena and rolled her out of the way as the sticks showered the tree trunk behind them.

"Cassandra, I swear!" Elena shouted. "I want to help you!"

"Then admit what you did!"

More branches split off, surging toward them. This was getting seriously out of hand. Abby removed the salt pendant from her neck, holding it in her fist. It wasn't much, but maybe it could keep Cassandra away from Elena long enough for them to escape.

"I didn't do anything," Elena shouted back.

This earned another surge of heavy debris charging toward them. Abby threw herself on the ground face first, and winced as something grazed her back. Elena cried in alarm—or pain.

Abby glanced up to find Elena leaning against the tree, clutching her arm. A single scratch lined her cheek, angry and red.

Abby shoved the mossy branch off her back and got to her feet, hurling her pendant at the heart of the swirling detritus. The wind stilled as sticks, rocks, and dried leaves clattered to the ground.

"Run!" Abby insisted, turning back to Elena. She grabbed the binoculars by Elena's feet, and scanned the area for her pendant.

"But—"

"I'm not sure how long we have. We have to run."

Pink stone glinted from muddy grass. Abby darted forward and closed her fingers around her necklace. Despite the mud and grime, she put it back around her neck. She felt oddly naked without it.

When she turned back to Elena, she had already gathered her fallen headphones and returned to the path, walking swiftly back to camp.

Abby followed, telling herself she wouldn't look back. That lasted about ten seconds. She glanced over her shoulder, peering through the binoculars. As Cassandra's ghost pulled itself back together, grainy and patchy, one thing was clear: she was furious.

Chapter Seventeen

Abby paced patiently while Mina examined Elena's scrapes and bruises. Well, as patiently as she could manage until her questions started spilling out and she was temporarily banished.

She went to the kitchen, fingers trembling as she reached for a mug. Wind howled outside, rain pouring down the window in sheets. Abby watched the storm twist the bushes, replaying Cassandra's attack in her mind.

She wondered if Cassandra's anger came from her need for justice, or if she had always had a temper, even when she was alive.

"Abby?"

She jumped, startled, and promptly relaxed when she saw it was Lucas. "What are you doing here?"

"Mina texted. She said Cassandra attacked you?"

Abby sighed. She picked up a pitcher and turned

on the faucet, watching the water slowly rise. "More like she attacked Elena and I happened to be there."

"Do you want to tell me what happened?"

"I just did. Cassandra thinks she followed Elena to her death. Elena swears she didn't go anywhere that night. Cassandra got angry and went all poltergeist on her."

"You had to use your gun on her?" Lucas sank into a chair at a nearby table.

Abby shook her head, turned off the tap as the water reached a decent level, and emptied it into the coffee maker. "I didn't have it with me."

"You brought Elena to her without the salt gun?" Lucas asked, his voice rising. He stopped, shaking his head, and added softly, "You didn't think you'd need it."

"She was friendly. Normal. Not aggressive." Abby scooped the grounds into the coffee maker. It whirled to life as she pressed the power button. "Every time we've spoken with her—everyone who's talked about her—she's seemed fine."

"No one's perfect."

Abby stiffened, unable to help but think of what he'd said about Chelsea. Was her ghost capable of doing what Cassandra had done? Surely not. Chelsea hadn't hurt anyone. Even when she was angry, she only ever raised her voice—never threw things or shoved anyone. Abby remembered her shouting at her mom once, when her parents had come home early because their dinner party had been canceled. Chelsea had thought she and Abby would have the house to themselves and she'd planned a whole romantic evening, with candles and everything—but when they heard the engine of her parents' car pulling into the driveway, she'd hardened into a frantic mess, cursing and blowing out candles as she stormed to the top of the banister and greeted her parents with furious shouts.

It was a memory Abby didn't like to think about. One she had all but forgotten.

"She wasn't perfect," Abby said softly, turning back to face Lucas.

"Yeah, but that still doesn't mean you could have anticipated her attacking someone like that."

"I meant Chelsea," Abby said. "You're right, she wasn't perfect."

Lucas leaned forward, lifting up his glasses to rub the bridge of his nose. "Like I said, no one's perfect."

"I remember now," Abby admitted. "She wasn't always a ray of sunshine. But most of the time, she was great."

Lucas smiled sadly. "That's all you can ask of anyone."

"I don't like to think about the bad parts."

"I know. And you don't need to. She was a really great person. I just don't want you to idolize her into someone that no one can live up to."

"Like Mina?"

Lucas nodded. "Mina's great too. I know you can't help but compare her to Chelsea sometimes, and that's okay—as long as you're thinking of human Chelsea and not 'glorified selective memory Chelsea.'"

It was good advice. She wondered if her memories hadn't been the only thing that had been glorified by time, but if her feelings had as well. She was certain the love she felt for Chelsea was real, but it wasn't constant joy. There were other feelings as well—disappointment when Chelsea missed a phone call or backed out of a date, and discomfort when Chelsea pressured her to cover for her while she got high or skipped English to work on her art project.

"And what about you?" Abby asked. "Any luck with Sabrina?"

He scratched his chin. "Not yet."

"Not yet? What are you waiting for? I let you team up with her for the walk so you could ask her."

"No, you teamed up with Nick so you could question him about Cassandra."

"Both things can be true," Abby pointed out. "So why the hesitation?"

Lucas folded his hands in his lap, shifting his weight. "It's just—things are good, you know. She laughs at my jokes. We like reading the same books. She's good with kids."

"But she might be a murderer?" Abby speculated. Even though Sabrina had been there that summer, she hadn't had a motive to kill Cassandra. And her arm had been broken, which would have made the actual killing part challenging.

Lucas flashed her a 'don't joke about that' look. "We work together."

Abby waited for Lucas to continue. When he didn't, she shrugged. "So? Mina and I work together."

"That's different. You two were dating before you worked together. If I ask Sabrina out and she says no, we're stuck together all summer and it'll be awkward."

"But if she says yes, then you get to see her every day for the rest of the summer."

"True." The fluorescent lights hummed above them, illuminating the wrinkles on Lucas's brow. "But if I wait until the last day of camp, then I don't have to worry about things being awkward. If it's meant to be, we'll make it work. If it isn't, we can go our separate ways."

Abby's chair squeaked as she slid back, shaking her head. She stood and filled two mugs with the freshly brewed coffee. "For what it's worth, I think you should ask her sooner rather than later. Want to see if Mina's had any breakthroughs with Elena?"

Lucas shook his head. "I've got to get back to watching the campers. Jason, Paxton, and Nick are working on something. With you and Elena gone, we're so low on staff I had to fake going to the bathroom to come see you."

"What are the guys working on?"

Lucas's chair squealed as he stood. "Beats me."

"See if you can find out," Abby called, carrying the mugs upstairs. She doubted it was important, but on the off chance it had anything to do with Cassandra's death, she wanted to know about it.

When she reached Mina's room, Mina's look of joy and relief made the trip worth it. She eagerly took the first mug and slipped a hand around Abby's waist, drawing her close and planting a soft kiss on her forehead. Abby's cheeks warmed at the attention, her heart fluttering. She wanted to stay here, breathing in Mina's nutty scent and relishing the feel of her strong protective arms around her waist—but Elena eyed her expectantly.

Abby placed the second mug of steaming coffee beside Elena, who took it with the world's smallest display of gratitude. The color had returned to her face and her mascara-coated eyes looked less puffy, so that was a start.

Abby kneeled beside her and asked gently, "Was Cassandra always quick to anger like that?"

"No," Elena said, then considered. "She would get upset, but not like that. She never hurt anyone."

Abby nodded. "I'm not sure she meant to hurt you. She seemed like she was angry and desperate for answers—but she was holding herself back. She wanted to scare you, not hurt you."

"Why?" Elena asked with a sob, setting her mug on the floor and hugging her knees to her chest. "I didn't do anything."

"Except sneak out the night she died."

Mina pinched the bridge of her nose, shaking her head as if she didn't approve of Abby continuing her investigation so quickly, but she made no move to stop her as she sank onto the foot of her bed and turned her attention to her coffee.

"Who did you meet in the woods that night?" Abby asked.

Elena stared at her black fingernails. "No one. I didn't go anywhere. I don't know why she said I did. Maybe she misremembered? She caught me sneaking out a few days before. We argued. She might have expected me to sneak out that night, but I didn't."

Abby considered this. While it was possible, it seemed unlikely Cassandra would misremember something that critical. She had said it had been storming. "When you snuck out previously, had it been raining?"

Elena shook her head. "No."

Abby ran her fingers through her hair. "Then that's not what Cassandra is remembering."

Elena gave Abby a pleading look. "Maybe—I don't know—maybe someone could have tricked her into thinking they were me?"

Mina's lips curled into an amused expression of disbelief. Abby agreed the theory was a bit far-fetched. "Why would someone do that?"

"I don't know!" Elena stood and paced the bedroom, arms crossed. The kittens meowed for her attention. Nibbles jumped onto her shoulder, trying to play with her hair. She gave a startled cry of alarm.

"Nibbles, no." Abby grabbed the kitten, holding him securely against her chest as he squirmed in protest. She took a seat on the wooden floor and placed the kitten in her lap, stroking his back until he purred. "Sorry about him. He loves to play."

Elena resumed pacing, her lips pressed together, eyebrows pinched. At last, she snapped her fingers. "Nick."

"What about him?"

"I bet he did it. He wanted to meet Cassandra, but knew she'd never follow him, so he must have left her a note, pretending to be me, to get her to agree to meet him."

"I haven't heard anything about a note," Mina interjected.

"Me neither," Abby said. "Cassandra said she followed you, not that you—or someone pretending to be you—lured her there."

"Well, maybe he bought a wig or a mask to disguise himself. Maybe he wasn't even trying to be me in particular, just someone—a camper—to get Cassandra to follow him."

"Why?" Abby asked. While she had to admit Nick did seem suspicious, luring Cassandra out to kill her seemed far too sinister for him.

Elena shrugged, her hands shaking. Desperation seeped through her voice. "Who knows? He wanted her alone with him? To try and win her back? To make her pay for breaking up with him."

Abby recalled the missing lost and found items and the purple plastic awareness bracelets on his wrist. If Cassandra had caught him stealing, that could be a stronger motive. "What do you know about his brother?"

Elena stiffened, confused about the question. "Jonathan? He's never been to camp. I met him once, at the funeral. He has cystic fibrosis."

"When was he diagnosed?"

"I don't know. A long time ago?"

"Before or after Cassandra died?"

Elena blinked. She bunched up the fabric of her hoodie and stared up at the ceiling as the harsh overhead light illuminated her mascara-stained cheeks. "I don't know."

"Cystic fibrosis is usually diagnosed young," Mina pointed out.

"What does this have to do with Cass?" Elena's voice came out dry and hoarse, making her sound young and vulnerable.

Knowing her strong dislike for Nick, Abby trod carefully. "Nick has been getting money for his brother in a way that Cassandra might not have approved of."

Elena's eyes narrowed. "Illegally?"

Abby shook her head, refusing to answer the question. "If he was, would Cassandra have turned him in?"

Elena's shoulders sagged as she bowed her head. "I don't know. Maybe? But she would have tried to talk him out of it first."

Mina's combat boots padded against the floor as she grabbed her sweater and headed toward the door. "I'm going to get some more coffee. Abby, come with me and I'll show you where the hot chocolate is."

Elena snorted, pulling her hands deeper into her hoodie. "Smooth. You could just say you want to talk about me behind my back."

"We do," Mina said bluntly. "But I also want coffee. Don't go anywhere until we get back."

Elena sank to her knees and picked up her mug, cupping it between both hands as Nibbles scrambled into her lap.

Abby followed Mina out into the hall and down the creaky stairs. "What do you think?"

"She's lying about not going out that night."

Abby studied her in surprise. "I think she's telling the truth. Her story isn't over the top and it's not changing. Liars tend to focus on too many small details, which leads them to get their story mixed up in the end."

"Where did you hear that?"

"It's in all the TV shows."

Mina sighed. "She could be an excellent liar."

"But it doesn't make sense," Abby stressed. "If she killed Cassandra, why is she so insistent that Cassandra was murdered? Wouldn't she *want* people to think she ran away?"

Mina's eyes filled with sympathy. "Maybe part of her blocked it out?"

"Maybe," Abby admitted, but she didn't think so. As much as Elena unnerved her, she didn't seem hostile.

"I think we need to face the facts," Mina said, opening the door to the kitchen. "Cassandra is sure she followed Elena out that night. Elena's denying that. That means she's guilty. She either killed her, or she met someone who did—and whoever this is, she thinks they are worth protecting more than her own sister."

Abby massaged her temples. If Elena had killed Cassandra—or knew who did—then she wouldn't have been the one pressing the police to look into the murder, or hurling accusations at Nick. Her sobs had felt real and raw, not staged. And Cassandra had admitted that she hadn't seen Elena's face—she was expecting Elena, so she could have easily seen someone else in the dark and assumed it was Elena. "Either way, we can't prove anything."

"No," Mina agreed. "I think it's time to start being extra careful. It's only a matter of time before the truth comes out. And someone would do anything to stop it. They've already killed once. What's to stop them from killing again?"

Chapter Eighteen

Mina's words echoed in Abby's mind as she returned to her cabin. After a cold shower, the thought faded long enough for her to get a good night's sleep, but returned as soon as she woke.

It was still dark out, with the faintest hint of dawn peeking over the trees. She checked her phone. It was almost 6 a.m., nearly an hour before her cabinmates would wake up. But she heard footsteps.

Her bunk creaked as she sat up and scanned the room. The sounds were coming from outside: they were unmistakably footsteps and…giggles?

Abby pulled a sweatshirt over her pajamas and slipped down the ladder. She tiptoed past half a dozen sleeping girls, and Elena, who snored gently, with her headphones on. As she reached the front window, it lit with the glow of a flashlight. She ducked until the footsteps passed and the light retreated. She forced herself to wait a few extra seconds before peeking through the window. Two counselors walked past the next cabin. The long blond hair and muscular shoulders were a dead giveaway for Jason. He wore dark hiking pants and a long-sleeved jacket open over a white T-shirt. His companion was obscured in the dark. She could barely make out the Camp Pine Whispers logo on the back of their shirt.

Abby considered they could be going for a run, but Jason was fidgeting. His fingers were scratching so hard at his jacket pocket, it was a miracle he hadn't worn a hole through it. Jason placed a hand on the other counselor's shoulder and guided them toward the woods. Light flickered across his jacket for a moment—just long enough for Abby to get a glimpse of the logo. Brevard College.

Abby's mind whirled trying to piece together where she had heard of that college lately. Hadn't that been where the Brazen Brushstrokes originated? If Jason had been a student there, did that mean he was part of that group? Elena could have been meeting him in the woods that night.

A pale, feminine figure stepped into the flashlight's rays. Abby barely recognized Hannah before she disappeared into the woods.

Her heart raced as she slipped on socks and shoes as quietly as possible and snuck out the front door, holding it until it shut softly behind her. Jason and Hannah were no longer in sight, but from the direction they had been heading, Abby had a pretty good idea which path they had gone down.

She texted Lucas—*Following Jason into the woods. He*

went to Brevard!—double-checked her phone was on silent, and stuffed it into her back pocket. If she was following a murderer/blackmailer into the woods, at least she was leaving a trail. She hoped there wouldn't be a need for anyone to follow it.

With a deep breath, she jogged across the twilight-lit campground, slowing only as she reached the trailhead. Twigs snapped under her sneakers. The branches darkened what little light she had to navigate by, so she ended up cupping her hand over her phone's light to guide her. She continued forward slowly, listening.

A light breeze whispered through the branches, rich with mossy earthy scents. Damp soil squelched under her sneakers, and she stumbled over several tree roots, catching herself on their dewy bark. Fallen branches littered the path, and the underbrush sparkled with rain-soaked leaves. How much of this damage was caused by the storm, and how much was caused by Cassandra?

After several minutes of walking, the soft glow of sunrise broke through the trees. She pocketed her phone and quickened her steps. Birds greeted one another, their morning chirps and songs filling the air. She had almost given up on finding Jason until she heard a voice ahead.

It was Jason's. She recognized his laid-back tone, but could only catch a few words. "About time… unless…do you think?"

Hannah responded enthusiastically. "It's gorgeous! I absolutely love it."

Crouching behind a tree, Abby peered around the trunk to find Hannah standing in a gazebo, marveling at the view. Or maybe the craftsmanship.

"You made this?"

"Yep."

Abby's heartbeat quickened. Was Jason still leading the Brazen Brushstrokes? All this time, had he kept the group going in secret?

"For *me?*"

"Kind of. It's so I could do this." Jason crouched down. For a second, Abby feared he was going to pull out a weapon, but it was only a box. With something small and shiny. That he extended toward Hannah as he asked, "Darling, will you marry me?"

Hannah's squeal of excitement sent several birds flying from the trees. Abby winced. She had felt fine sneaking up on Jason when she thought he had been up to something sinister, but watching Hannah throw herself into Jason's open arms, she suddenly felt she was intruding.

Her foot caught on a twig, which cracked loudly in the quiet of the forest. Hannah and Jason's gaze turned to her at once, but instead of fear or anger, there was only joy. Hannah flashed her engagement ring.

"Oh, Abby, *look!*" She ran toward Abby with her finger held out. "Can you believe it? Jason proposed. I'm engaged!"

Abby forced a smile. "Congratulations."

"And look, he built this whole gazebo by himself! Isn't that amazing?"

"Paxton and Nick helped," Jason admitted, nodding toward the gazebo.

It was indeed a beautiful sight. She hoped Cassandra's ghost didn't tear it up.

Chapter Nineteen

Word of Jason and Hannah's engagement spread quickly. There was even a cake with their initials drawn in sprinkles served with lunch, and a party accompanied by hand-painted declarations of love strung between trees. The counselors dressed up—Paxton and Nick wore proper button-down shirts and Sabrina wore a black dress complete with a set of pearls. Elena was the only one who stuck to their usual outfit—denim shorts and dark hoodie.

"I need to talk to Cass again," Elena insisted, hovering directly behind Abby as she tried to enjoy her slice of cake at the makeshift engagement party.

Abby shook her head, watching the campers gather in the grass around a projector showcasing photos of Jason and Hannah. Lucas slid up to Sabrina's side and she placed her hand in his, softly kissing his cheek. Abby internally cheered. He had finally asked her out! And she had said yes. Everyone—except Elena—

seemed in good spirits. There was a warm, jovial vibe in the air that hinted good times lay ahead. "Not until we figure out what happened. It's too dangerous."

"But she needs to know I'm telling the truth."

Abby gave her a look of sympathy. "I don't think it's going to be that easy. Until we can prove to her that you weren't there that night, I'm not sure talking is going to help."

Elena's fists clenched at her sides. "Then I'll prove it."

As Elena stormed across the clearing, laughter and cheers floated behind her. Abby glanced to where Jason was sitting, his arm draped over Hannah. They were both grinning so widely, Abby bet their cheeks would hurt the next day. She searched the crowd for Mina and found her chatting with Carol and Paxton, the breeze making her long dress ripple around her legs. She looked so at ease here, mingling with the staff, munching on cheese and fruit. A warmth fluttered through Abby as she was reminded that Mina had taken this job for her—to spend time with her. It was followed by a wave of guilt that Abby had spent the past few weeks obsessing over Cassandra's murder instead of giving Mina the quality time she deserved.

"What was that about?" Lucas carefully cradled his Rice Krispie treat as he joined Abby at the edge of the pavilion.

A trickle of guilt sank into the pit of her stomach as she asked, "Do you think Mina's having a good time?"

Lucas glanced at her quizzically, then followed her

gaze to where Mina laughed boldly at something Carol had said. "Sure seems like it to me."

Abby scuffed her sneakers through the dirt, trying her best to shove her guilt from her mind as she turned to face Lucas. "When were you going to tell me you asked Sabrina out?"

Lucas scratched the back of his neck. "Actually, she asked me—last night when she came to return my book."

"You make a cute couple," Abby said, genuinely meaning it.

"Yeah, but she returned my book with the corner bent, so—" Lucas was grinning widely enough that Abby knew he was teasing. She gently elbowed him, shaking her head.

"Seriously though," he said, his voice tightening. "What was Elena upset about?"

Abby watched Elena scowl at the partygoers from the shade at the edge of the woods. "Cassandra thinks Elena was there the night she died, but Elena swears she wasn't."

"And you believe her?"

Abby shrugged. "She seems to mean it. Mina thinks she could be protecting someone."

"Who?"

"Jason? Paxton? Anyone, really."

Lucas eyed Jason, who was wrapping his arms further around Hannah. He kissed her cheek and the campers burst into a round of cheers and applause followed by the nursery rhyme that Hannah and Jason were sitting in a tree, K-I-S-S-I-N-G. Jason egged them on by kissing Hannah on the lips at the conclusion.

Lucas shook his head. "I don't know. I got the feeling he was up to something, but this whole engagement thing seems to be it. He doesn't really give me 'killer in the woods' vibes, once you get past the initial appearance."

"That would explain what he was doing with the toolbox." Abby eyed the gazebo. It was impressive work to have been built so quickly.

"And the mystery of my missing paints," Lucas added, pointing to the signs. "I just hope he didn't throw them out after he finished."

"At least one mystery is solved." So the missing paint and the abandoned house weren't connected after all. She'd spent weeks trying to track down Cassandra's killer, and all she had done was stir up more mysteries and questions. Maybe it was time to take a break. To focus on Mina, at least for the duration of the party, until her counselor duties kicked back in. She stepped toward Mina. "I think I'm going to catch up with my girlfriend."

"Good idea!" Lucas called after her, turning back to the crowd. Out of the corner of her eye, she saw him heading toward Sabrina.

Sunlight brought out subtle shades of brown in Mina's long hair, which fell slightly past her shoulders to the middle of her form-fitting denim blue dress. Small floral patches decorated the collar and sleeves, so well placed Abby would have thought the dress had come that way if she hadn't seen Mina attach them herself. As Abby slipped her hands around Mina's waist, she found the fabric softer than expected. It was warm and inviting, imbued with Mina's usual nutty scent, sunscreen, and a new beachy fragrance.

"Hey." Mina pulled Abby closer and greeted her with a quick kiss to the forehead. Abby assumed that was to keep the kids from starting another round of the kissing song. It worked. Although that may have had more to do with the popsicles and bubbles Carol was handing out, and less to do with Mina's self-restraint. "Paxton and I were just talking about white water rafting. Have you been?"

"Not recently," Abby said. "I went a couple of times as a kid."

"There's apparently a few great places to go around here, if you think you could find the time—"

"Yes." Abby pressed herself against Mina's side, resting her head against Mina's shoulder. "On my next day off, let's go."

"Are you sure?" Mina lowered her voice, eyes darting between Abby and Paxton.

Paxton took the hint that she wanted to speak to Abby privately, for he feigned a cough and went to get some water, even though his cup wasn't empty. Still, she was relieved to have a bit of privacy as she and Mina inched further from the crowd, until they were bathed in the shade of close-knit trees.

"What about Cassandra?" Mina asked.

"She can wait." Abby touched the back of Mina's hand almost instinctively, as if their fingers belonged together. When Mina didn't make a move to take her hand, she let it fall back to her side. "Honestly, my mind keeps spinning in circles. I think maybe taking a break would do some good, so I can come back to it with a fresh perspective. We're halfway through the summer and I've hardly spent any time with you."

"Yeah." Mina's rings clinked as she brushed a strand of hair behind her ear. She folded her arms across her chest. "I can't say I'm happy about that. But I get it."

"I'm sorry," Abby said, truly regretting that she hadn't made Mina more of a priority.

"White water rafting," Mina said, holding out her pinky finger. "Our next date, promise?"

"Rain or shine," Abby said, intertwining her pinky with Mina's. "Pinky promise."

"I don't know about rain." Mina bit back a grin, her eyes sparkling in a way that made Abby's heart flutter. She loved that a single look from Mina could make her feel wanted and appreciated and attractive all at once. "I think we might need a backup plan."

"Pillow fort?" Abby suggested. "Indoor camping?"

Mina pulled her close, her warm palms pressing into the small of Abby's back, nose grazing her ear as she whispered, "As long as I get you all to myself for a few hours, I'm happy."

Abby's heart soared. She wanted nothing more than to tangle her fingers in Mina's hair and kiss her until she was breathless. She whispered, "Me too."

"Abby!" Lucas's shout reminded her that they weren't alone—and in fact many of the things she had been thinking of doing with Mina were far too inappropriate to do in front of a crowd.

She slipped from Mina's grip until only their hands brushed, their fingers intertwining as if they were made to fit together, as they headed toward Lucas, who was waving them over. He stood at the edge of the gazebo with Jason, Hannah, Sabrina, and Nick.

"I was just asking them about the abandoned house in the woods," Lucas said, as Abby and Mina drew near. "Nick thinks he's seen it before."

Nick adjusted his baseball cap. "Our first year as counselors, we were hanging out in the woods one night. You know—" He gestured taking a swig from an imaginary bottle. "Having a good time. We heard someone coming, so we ran to hide. We all split up. Remember, Sabrina? You and I ended up in some abandoned house. We had a good time." He winked.

Sabrina blushed, folding her arms across her chest. "I must have blocked that out of my memory because, ew, Nick, it wasn't like that—we just made out a little."

Lucas stiffened, his fist clenching as he shook his head in Nick's direction with a glare that made Abby wonder if he was imagining beating him up. Not that Lucas would ever beat anyone up—he'd been the only student in their high school to fail the self-defense portion of their PE class because he refused to fight the training officer and instead philosophized about the immorality of violence. But the way he looked at Nick, he certainly seemed to be reconsidering his views on the matter.

Elena stepped out of the shade. "Did Cassandra know about this?"

Abby turned, surprised to find her eavesdropping. They hadn't been whispering, but they hadn't been talking loud enough for her to hear across the clearing. She had somehow crept up on them.

Nick turned to her with a soft shake of his head. "We'd broken up. It wasn't any of her business. And she wouldn't have cared anyway."

"What about you, Sabrina?" Elena whirled to Sabrina, rage across her face. "Were you jealous of Cassandra?"

Sabrina's glossy pink lips parted in surprise. Her earrings scattered sunlight as she shook her head. "Of course not. I wasn't into Nick like that. It was just a fling."

"It was just a fling," Lucas repeated, voice dripping with relief.

"Are you sure about that?" Elena demanded, advancing on Sabrina. "Because I remember the morning we found out Cass went missing, your hair was *wet*."

"Because I'd showered." Sabrina glanced around at the others, as if searching for signs that they agreed these accusations were absurd. She took a small step back from Elena, inching toward Lucas's side.

Elena's eyes flashed. Lucas put his arm out in front of Sabrina. Elena took that as an opportunity to round on Nick. "And you," she said heatedly. "Your shoes were *soaked*."

"We've been over this before," Sabrina said, exasperation slipping through. "The campground was covered in mud and puddles. You've got to stop accusing us of all of this. It's not healthy."

"When did you find the house?" Abby asked quickly, before Elena could say something she regretted. "Before or after Cassandra went missing?"

"I don't know," Sabrina said dismissively. "How am I supposed to remember?"

"Before." Nick looked thoughtful. "Maybe a week or two? Cassandra found the drinks, remember? We were all upset with her. She threatened to get Paxton kicked out."

"What?" Abby turned to where Paxton was picking up discarded paper cups. When he'd mentioned that some people had been found drinking, he'd conveniently left out the fact that Cassandra had found *him*. His gaze met Abby's and he tossed the cups into the nearest trash bag before jogging to her side.

"We were just talking—" Abby began.

"Cassandra threatened to get you kicked out," Elena said, cutting to the chase.

Paxton's eyes widened, his face taking on a guilty expression as he slipped his hands into his pockets. "It wasn't a big deal. We argued and then we made up the day before she— disappeared."

Abby could tell he almost said 'died' but caught himself. She wanted to believe him, but leaving this out made him look pretty suspicious. "Getting kicked out of your own camp is a pretty big deal."

"She just threatened to tell my parents," Paxton explained.

"Who would have thrown you out," Elena added. "You know they would have, don't deny it. And besides, you keep saying you made up—but can anyone back this up? Did any of you see this?"

The other counselors exchanged uncomfortable glances.

Slowly, the rest of the group shook their heads. An air of suspicion built around Paxton. But Paxton had talked with Cassandra's ghost. Surely she would have been more upset if he had done something to anger her. Unless Paxton had been the one filled with anger, while Cassandra thought everything was smoothed over between them. He knew Elena was involved with the Brazen Brushstrokes and that Cassandra was worried about her sneaking out. He could have disguised himself as Elena and lured Cassandra to her death. Abby gulped.

"That's what I thought," Elena said bitterly. "She was going to get you kicked out of camp. But you're still here and Cassandra is *dead*." She slammed a fist on the nearest table and leaned toward Paxton. "To think, all this time I trusted you!"

Paxton's eyes widened. "Elena, I— wait!"

Elena stormed out of the clearing and into the forest's shade, heading back toward camp.

Paxton glanced at Nick with a pleading expression. "You know I had nothing to do with Cass—"

"We know, man." Nick nodded in solidarity. "Give it time, she'll come around."

Sabrina took a deep, shuddering breath and turned to Jason with a sympathetic look, eyes threatening to spill tears. "I'm sorry, Jason. This is supposed to be a happy day for you and Hannah."

"It's alright," Jason said with a shrug. "We all miss Cassandra. Without knowing what happened to her, it's tough. I wish we could get some closure."

Nick hung his head. "We all do, man. We all do."

Sabrina leaned into Lucas as he draped an arm protectively over her shoulder. "I just hope wherever she is, she's happy."

Paxton glanced at Abby. His gaze reminded her that he knew exactly where Cassandra was and that it was up to Abby to bring her the peace her spirit longed for.

Abby nodded in agreement, her chest pounding. She wished she could trust him, but she feared he'd just become her top suspect.

Chapter Twenty

Abby wasn't sure if it was the cake or the excitement that caused most of the campers to hit their beds before the lights went out, but she took the win. The few remaining kids settled in as Elena counted down from ten and shut off the overhead lights, leaving them in darkness broken by dappled moonlight.

Abby shut her eyes and found herself on the stairs of the abandoned house, voices drifting from down below. Cassandra floated in the doorway, haunting and ghostly, as if she were from some children's cartoon. Someone was sobbing, repeating that they were sorry. Abby peered further over the railing to see Paxton and Elena standing side by side. She couldn't tell which of them was responsible for the gut-wrenching sobs.

From somewhere behind her, a voice whispered her name. "Abby!"

Abby was jolted awake by a very real voice whispering in her ear, a very solid hand on her shoulder.

She opened her eyes, dazed. It was still dark, but the moonlight had moved from the foot of her bed to fall across the top of Lilly's bunk. It was empty.

She turned in a panic that was quickly soothed as she saw the young girl at the edge of her bed. *She* had been the one shaking Abby awake.

"Lilly?" Abby whispered, reaching for her phone. The screen showed that she had once again forgotten to charge it, the battery on three percent. It was shortly after midnight.

Abby turned back to Lilly and asked, "Do you need to go to the bathroom?"

Lilly shook her head. Her unkempt blonde hair brushed Abby's blankets as she leaned forward and whispered. "She snuck out."

"Who?"

"Elena."

Abby sat up and confirmed Elena's bunk was empty. An unsettling feeling rose in her stomach. She tried to remain calm for Lilly. "She probably just went to the bathroom."

Lilly shook her head. "She climbed onto your bunk, looking for something. She woke me up, but I pretended to be asleep. She took something. I thought she would go back to sleep, so I opened my eyes and I saw her putting on her shoes. She kept looking at you like she was afraid you'd wake up. Then she took her backpack, and snuck out."

Abby felt a growing unease as she rummaged

around the foot of her bed and felt only blankets. Her briefcase, containing the ghost-hunting equipment, wasn't there. Elena must have taken it. She almost swore, but recalled Lilly's eyes so close to hers.

"What are we going to do?" Lilly asked excitedly, as if this were some fun game of hide and seek and not a potential murderer stealing the only way to communicate with the victim.

Abby held up her finger, indicating to give her a minute as she fumbled in the dark, until she pulled on a hoodie and stuffed her phone, a flashlight, and a pair of socks into the pouch. The ladder creaked as she descended her bunk. If Elena had taken her ghost supplies, that could only mean she was going back to face Cassandra. Considering what happened last time, there was no telling what Cassandra would do. And Elena didn't know the first thing about ghosts—if Cassandra attacked her, she would be defenseless. Abby needed to find her and stop her before she got seriously hurt.

Abby tiptoed across the cabin and slipped into a pair of sneakers, wishing Elena hadn't been so foolish. She wondered if Lucas was right—if bringing Paxton to meet Cassandra's ghost had been a bad idea. That was what had gotten them into this mess in the first place. Elena would never have known about Cassandra's ghost otherwise.

The sound of Velcro tore her out of her thoughts, and she turned to see Lilly putting on sneakers.

Abby put a comforting hand on her shoulder. "Go back to bed."

"I want to help."

"It's too dangerous."

Lilly folded her arms across her cat-themed pajama shirt and countered, "Staying here without an adult is dangerous."

Abby sighed, and sent a text to Lucas saying she was following Elena into the woods. She then opened her texts with Mina to say the same thing, and ask if Mina could come and watch the campers while she was away, but her battery died before she could press send.

She stared at the black screen, pressing the side buttons, trying everything she could to get it to wake up. After several seconds of prolonged darkness, she turned to Lilly and whispered, "Okay. How about I take you to the Lodge? You go in and get Mina, and tell her what you told me. Then bring her back here until I get back, alright?"

"Alright." Lilly dove back to her sneakers enthusiastically.

Abby held a finger to her lip, reminding her to be quiet as she slowly—and quietly—fastened Lilly's shoes. The last thing she wanted was her entire cabin wanting to go on a midnight field trip. "Let's be quiet, okay?"

As Lilly nodded, Abby watched the dark bunks for signs of movement. When she was confident none of the other girls were awake, she opened the door as slowly as possible. It still creaked louder than she would have liked, but not enough to interrupt any patterns of gentle snoring coming from inside.

Holding the door as wide as she dared, Abby

ushered Lilly outside and followed. The door shut behind them with a quiet *click*.

A chilly breeze combed through their hair, rustling the nearby trees. An owl hooted somewhere in the distance. Abby held Lilly's hand as she led her down the small dirt path by memory, waiting until they were a few yards away from the cabin before she risked turning on the flashlight. Even then, she kept the rays directed at the dirt trail in front of them, careful not to shine it on any cabin windows.

Starlight twinkled in the sky, sparkling off the lake to their right and illuminating the outline of the mountains to their left. If she hadn't been worried about Elena confronting Cassandra, she would have savored a leisurely stroll across the peaceful campgrounds. Instead, she found herself walking briskly, imagining all the ways Elena's encounter could go wrong. At least she knew Elena was likely headed to the spot where she had last met Cassandra.

The walk to the Lodge felt like it took far longer than usual, even though they followed the same path. She was relieved when the building finally loomed before them. The front door was locked. Abby tried knocking, then resorted to shining a flashlight directly on Mina's window. She waved until Mina appeared in her oversized sleeping shirt, hair frizzy, with a disgruntled expression, wincing from the light. Eventually, her eyes widened in recognition and concern. Abby pointed at the front door. Mina straightened and turned toward the hall, disappearing from sight.

Abby led Lilly back to the front door and waited,

bouncing lightly on her feet. Every second that passed was another second Cassandra could hurt Elena. She turned to Lilly and said, "Mina will be here any second —" She paused, hoping Mina would open the door right then. When she didn't, she continued, "Can you wait here until she gets here?"

Lilly looked uncertain, but nodded, chewing her fingernails.

"Okay. It'll just be a second," Abby promised, running back down the path, toward the forest. She felt guilty leaving Lilly there all alone, but the camp was safe. What had happened to Cassandra had been a one-time thing. Whoever had killed her had clearly had a vendetta against her—either she caught them doing something wrong or they lured her out in the middle of the night to kill her. Abby's footsteps slowed.

Was that what Elena was doing to her now? Luring her out into the woods to kill her like she had Cassandra?

Nearing the bottom of the hill, Abby glanced back to see Mina standing in the doorway, ushering Lilly inside. She let out a sigh of relief that at least they were safe, as she turned to face the woods.

The woods where Cassandra had died after following Elena.

Her flashlight illuminated the path between large trees with twisting branches that rustled and swayed in the growing wind. Damp pine needles crunched under her sneakers. She slowed her steps to quiet them, and continued deeper, until the air grew thick and musky, signaling she was in the heart of the forest.

She stepped through a spider's web and shivered, unable to shake the silky strands entirely from her skin —just like she couldn't quite shake the feeling that this was a trap. Covering the top of her flashlight, she proceeded with caution, letting out just enough light to keep her from tripping over stones and tree roots, but not enough to be seen from far ahead. Every few steps, she covered the light entirely and paused to listen.

Other than whispering trees and the occasional animal cry, the forest was quiet. Eerie, as if it was waiting for something.

Abby was both relieved and disappointed when she reached the place Elena had last seen Cassandra. There was no sign of her. Hand still cupped over her flashlight, she let a few slender beams of light guide her forward, taking small quiet steps, until she saw a sign of life—a faint yellow light between the trees above the rocky slope.

Abby paused at the base, turned off her flashlight, and listened.

Voices drifted down, faint and muffled at first, growing steadily louder. Abby held her breath as she crept closer, wincing at every crunch and squelch her sneakers made.

"—sure she gave those to you?" a soft, masculine voice asked. Abby had a hard time picturing who it belonged to, but it certainly wasn't Elena or Cassandra.

"Yes," a curt, feminine voice responded. That *could* be Elena.

"You didn't steal them?"

"I'm going to bring them back as soon as I talk to Cass." *Definitely* Elena.

"That's still stealing." A flashlight's rays swayed dangerously toward Abby before striking through the sky above. When Abby risked glancing up, she saw that the figure speaking had been Paxton, and he'd tucked his flashlight into an armpit while his hands were folded across his chest.

Paxton was working with Elena? She pictured them meeting here, ten years ago, with Cassandra crouched in the shadows, just like Abby was now. What had they been discussing to have gotten her killed? Abby sucked in a breath, trying to keep quiet as she inched forward, straining to listen.

Paxton's flashlight spilled over Elena, giving Abby a clear view of her profile. She was peeking through the binoculars with a deep frown. While Elena wore her usual jeans and dark hoodie, Paxton was dressed in a T-shirt, sweatpants, and sneakers. It took Abby a moment to realize why he looked so different. His lack of accessories, messy curls, and sleepy expression made him look like he had been woken up rather than stayed up late planning this excursion.

"It's borrowing," Elena said with a heated breath. "Shut up and let me focus."

"Oh yeah, keep pressing all the buttons and break it."

"Don't tell me what to do."

Neither of them bothered keeping their voice down. Abby took this as a sign they hadn't seen her and didn't expect her to be lurking nearby. Emboldened by the thought, she crept up the rocky mountainside. The rock was cold and rough against her palms, difficult to navigate with only a sliver of moonlight. But if she was careful, she could crawl to the top.

The wind picked up, showering Abby in dirt. She winced and increased her grip as she tried to keep her balance. A few tiny raindrops sprinkled her skin. She hoped the skies weren't about to open into a downpour. The last thing she needed was rain to drown out their conversation.

Above, something snapped.

Elena cursed.

Paxton let out a loud sigh. "See."

"I can fix it," Elena insisted, her voice desperate.

Abby's muscles protested as she climbed faster, pulling herself to the edge of the clearing to see what damage Elena had done. Abby pictured the binoculars lying shattered, her only way to communicate with ghosts gone forever.

As Paxton's flashlight illuminated Elena, relief washed over her. Elena was examining the walkie-talkie and antenna attachment, clearly looking for some sign of how they fit together.

"It wraps around the antenna," Abby supplied, causing both of them to jump and turn toward her in surprise.

Paxton momentarily blinded her with his flashlight. She scrambled the rest of the way onto the grassy clearing by touch alone until Paxton lowered the flashlight with an apology.

"What are you doing here?" Elena demanded.

"What are *you* doing?" Abby countered.

Elena pointed the tip of the walkie-talkie at Paxton. "Trying to get him to confess."

Paxton folded his arms across his chest. "Confess what? That I'm terrible at functioning on two hours' sleep?"

"That you killed her!" Elena's voice trembled.

Abby couldn't tell if she was about to punch Paxton or break down in a fit of tears. She moved forward cautiously, trying to keep Elena calm. "Why don't you hand me the walkie-talkie and we can sit down and talk about this?"

"No!" Elena's fists clenched around the equipment. Abby sucked in a breath, fearing she might break the antenna. Instead, Elena stepped toward Paxton and slammed the walkie-talkie against his chest. "You've gotten away with this for too long."

"Whoa." Paxton stumbled back, hands in the air. "Elena, chill."

Elena continued forward, dropping the equipment to grab the front of his hoodie. "Cassandra needs to know the truth. *I* need to know the truth."

Rain descended. Abby heard a sound like a swarm of insects growing louder until she could see the rain falling in sheets across the clearing seconds before cold drops battered her skin. She considered running to the protection of a nearby tree, but the rain was the least of her worries as Elena was thrown off Paxton, as if yanked back by invisible strings. She hovered in the air, kicking helplessly at an attacker that couldn't be seen.

Cassandra.

Abby's heart raced. If Paxton had really killed Cassandra, there was no telling what she would do to him.

Paxton cried out in alarm, reaching for Elena, but she was thrown across the clearing, landing on a grassy patch, dangerously close to the cliff's edge.

"Wait," Abby called. Cassandra wasn't going after Paxton. She was trying to protect him—from Elena. "She's just trying to help!"

Paxton ran toward Elena, and she glared at him. "S-stop—" she choked, tears filling her eyes. She pointed a wavering hand at Paxton. "H-he—"

"Oh, come on!" Paxton shouted into the dark. "Elena didn't kill you, Cass! And neither did I!"

Abby didn't have time to think about whether she believed him or not. She scrambled to find the fallen walkie-talkie. If they could get Cassandra to talk to them, get her to calm down, maybe she could make amends with Elena. She turned on her flashlight, letting its pale beams coat the rain-soaked ground until the walkie-talkie gleamed in a patch of ferns.

Elena's gasps grew louder and more desperate as she pried at invisible fingers around her neck.

"Cassandra!" Abby called, setting her flashlight down to pick up the walkie-talkie. She ran her fingers through the grass, feeling for the missing antenna. "You're hurting her!"

"I know you're upset," Paxton added. "But Elena needs to be able to breathe to listen."

The wind swelled, splattering Abby in even colder bursts of rain. Was it just her imagination or had the temperature dropped? All she knew for sure was that Elena was turning red, struggling for air, and Cassandra wasn't letting her go.

"Damn it." Abby shoved the walkie-talkie into her pocket, abandoning the missing antenna, and ran to her briefcase. Finding the salt gun was more important. "We don't want to hurt you, Cassandra. We just want to talk."

Abby didn't like using the salt gun. She wasn't sure if ghosts could feel pain or not, but it weakened them. And it was creepy, watching them disperse into fragments as if they were sand. But Cassandra was hurting Elena, and Abby couldn't think of another way to stop her.

Relief washed over her as she saw the bronze handle of the gun sticking out of a pocket in the briefcase. Her palm closed around the cold metal as she picked it up and pointed it toward Elena.

"Wait!" Paxton shouted. "Don't hurt her!"

Abby couldn't risk Elena suffocating any longer. She pulled the trigger, sending a blast of salt into the night. It burst in front of Elena, showering her in a cloud of salt that quickly melted in the rain. Elena fell to the ground, gasping and sputtering, then coughing.

Paxton was at her side in an instant, his hand on her shoulder. "Are you alright?"

"Fine." Elena scooted away from him. "Don't touch me!"

Paxton pulled his hand away, raising it up in a sign of surrender. He said softly, "I didn't hurt her, Elena. I promise. You know I wouldn't."

Elena scowled at him, blinking back tears as she traced the faded scratch on her cheek.

Beams from Abby's fallen flashlight captured Paxton's concerned expression as he turned toward her. "What about Cassandra?"

"She'll be fine," Abby said, ninety percent certain that was true. "Salt stuns them. It might take her a while to be able to speak with us again. And she might be upset. But it takes more than a little salt to get rid of a ghost."

When Paxton continued to stare apprehensively into the rain, Abby added, "Trust me. I've sent my fair share of ghosts on. We'll know when she's gone."

The wind shifted, spraying more rain into Abby's face. Heavy drops pattered against the leaves protecting them from the worst of the rain, but the group was already damp and dripping. Thunder rumbled in the distance.

Elena started to stand and fell, letting out a very un-Elena like whimper.

"What's wrong?" Paxton asked, shielding his eyes from the rain as he squinted at her.

"My ankle." Elena hesitated before unzipping the side of her boot. She pulled down her sock, letting raindrops trickle over her skin as she moved her foot into the light. Abby didn't see any signs of damage, but Elena said, "I must have twisted it when I fell."

"May I—?" Paxton reached out hesitantly. When Elena made no move to stop him, he placed his hand gently on her ankle. She hissed in pain. He immediately let go. "It's swollen. Can you walk back?"

Elena nodded, leaning against him as he helped her to her feet. Either she had changed her mind about him being capable of murder or her pain was so bad she didn't care. She took a few steps and stopped, wincing. "It really hurts."

"Wait here," Paxton suggested. "I'll run back to camp and get a golf cart. You'll have to climb down to the main path. Can you do that?"

Elena chewed her lower lip. "Just hurry."

Abby spied her briefcase in the next flash of lightning and scrambled to it. Thankfully, it was latched shut, rain pounding the casing instead of the equipment inside.

The ground trembled, thunder roaring at a bolt of lightning ripped across the sky. Paxton turned back and shouted, "Are you sure you're going to be okay out here?"

"We should get inside," Abby called back, clutching the briefcase to her chest. "The house I told you about isn't far from here. We could carry Elena there."

"I can hobble," Elena protested.

Paxton was already running back to them. He kneeled in a patch of moss beside Elena. "Climb onto my back. It'll go faster."

"I'm not a child," Elena grumbled. But she was already putting her arms around his neck.

Paxton stood. "Lead the way."

Chapter Twenty-One

Wind howled as they reached the house, sending sheets of rain sideways. Abby pulled back the tarp and opened the unlatched window, before scrambling inside. She ran to the front door and lifted the iron deadbolt. The door slammed open in the wind, pounding against the peeling wallpaper as rain darkened the floor.

Elena slid off Paxton's back, wincing. She turned to him with a weak smile. "Thanks."

Abby unfolded the metal chair in the corner and held it out for Elena. She stepped back, wringing out her wet hair and wishing she had a dry set of clothes to change into—or at least a fire to warm herself beside. One glance at the fireplace showed that lighting a fire was probably not a good idea. Besides the fact that they didn't have firewood, it looked like it hadn't been used in a hundred years.

Paxton wiped rain from his forehead. "No problem. Sit tight. I'll be back with that golf cart."

"You don't need to go out in this," Elena countered, her voice softer now. Abby wondered if she was feeling sorry for dragging him out here in the middle of the night and accusing him of murder. She hoped she was. Some remorse would do her good. "You can wait until the storm dies down."

Paxton was already reaching for the door handle, his shoulders stiff with resolve. "It's just rain. I'll be back in no time."

He swung the door open, the storm's howl growing louder as he stepped out into the night.

"Be careful!" Elena called, her voice strained.

Abby shut the door behind him. The stiff silence that followed was soon broken by a clap of thunder. The storm grew louder, a constant, drumming presence that pressed in on all sides. Elena stared out the window, her breath fogging the glass.

Abby felt the night's exhaustion catch up to her. She focused on the red light of the camera blinking above them. It made her feel uneasy, not knowing who had planted that camera.

She could worry about that later—when she was back at camp, safely tucked in Mina's arms, dry and warm and comfortable. For now, she just had to wait until Paxton returned.

Elena looked through the binoculars and lowered them with a look of disappointment. She and Paxton both seemed to care about Cassandra. They were kind, compassionate people—she wanted to believe they were innocent. But someone had killed Cassandra. And Cassandra had seen Elena. That meant she had to know something. "Elena, I know you don't think you had anything to do with Cassandra's death, but—"

Elena stiffened. "I told you, I didn't—"

"Hear me out," Abby said, holding up a hand. "Whatever you were doing that night, whoever you visited—I get it, you're trying to protect them. But even if they didn't hurt Cassandra, they might know *something*."

"I didn't visit anyone," Elena insisted, her voice cracking. "I never left the cabin, I swear!"

"Then why would Cassandra say she saw you?"

"I don't know!" Elena cried. "That's why I wanted to talk to her. To see what she meant."

Elena's defenses seemed to be down, but she was stubbornly sticking to her story. Perhaps she had felt such guilt over the role she may have played in Cassandra's death that she lied to herself all these years, she convinced herself that her story was real. There must be some way to get through to her, to prove that remembering would help Cassandra.

Abby sucked in a deep breath. "I lost someone too, you know. Her name was Chelsea. She was my girl-friend. She was also one of my best friends."

Elena's eyes softened. "I'm sorry."

"She died in a car accident, on her way to see a movie that I'd invited her to see."

Elena leaned forward, staring intently at Abby.

"For years, I blamed myself." Abby let out a shaky breath before forcing herself to continue. If she could connect to Elena, maybe she could get her to open up. "Part of me still does. In an odd way, I think it makes me feel more in control, you know? Like, if I had done something differently, I could have stopped the accident. So, as long as I don't go to any more movie theaters, no one else will die. It's not rational, I know, but it made me feel like I had control over something I don't."

Elena chewed her lower lip, eyes glistening with tears. "I've blamed myself, too. For Cassandra's death. I keep thinking if I'd just apologized, or stayed by her side, maybe she'd still be here."

Abby felt a pang of sympathy, but she pressed on, even though she could feel the tight knot of grief forming in her chest again. "Is it possible, though…that you've convinced yourself you didn't leave that night, because it's easier that way? That it's less painful to pretend it didn't happen?"

Elena's gaze hardened. "I've gone over every detail in my head, wondering if I could have done something. But that night, I was in *bed*. Asleep. I swear, I'm telling the truth."

"Okay." Abby swallowed, trying to keep her rising frustration from showing. "Let's think about this. If you saw someone sneaking out in the middle of the night, in a storm like this, would you be able to recognize them?"

"Maybe." Elena hesitated. "I mean, depending on who it was—maybe?"

"What about someone who didn't want to be found? Someone sneaking out would be trying to keep their identity hidden as much as possible, right? Maybe Cassandra saw someone sneaking out and assumed it was you because she had been expecting it."

Elena's breath caught. "But then we're back at square one. It could have been anyone!"

Abby thought for a moment, picturing everyone at camp who could possibly be mistaken for a teenage Elena wearing a hoodie in the dark. "Not anyone. Jason would have been too tall."

"I guess."

"And Carol and Paxton were at the Lodge," Abby continued.

"Paxton was staying in the cabins," Elena said, then sighed. Abby couldn't tell if the sound came from anguish or relief. "But he was in cabin one."

Abby considered that for a moment, then nodded. "Whoever was sneaking out must have been in cabin three to seven, otherwise they wouldn't have passed cabin two, where Cassandra saw them."

"That means it had to be—"

A floorboard creaked. Abby turned toward the sound in time to see someone dart back from the doorway in the kitchen.

They weren't alone.

Chapter Twenty-Two

"Who's there?" Elena snapped, straightening from where she had been sitting by the window. She hobbled to her feet—well, foot—and braced herself against the wall. "We have a gun!"

Abby turned to Elena in fear before realizing that Elena was looking at *her* gun—the salt gun, which was about as harmful against people as pepper spray. Before Abby had time to explain this, Sabrina stepped out of the kitchen, her hands raised over her head, face pale with fright.

"Don't shoot," she said quickly. "It's just me!"

Abby let out a sigh of relief before her suspicion returned. What was Sabrina doing in this abandoned house? She was dressed in a sweater, yoga pants, and hiking boots—far less put together than her usual outfits. Her hair was pulled into a ponytail, damp strands sticking to her neck. Without her usual makeup, she looked softer and more vulnerable. Abby could have mistaken her for a camper.

"What are you doing here?" Elena asked.

"Sorry, I didn't mean to eavesdrop." Her pink fingernails gleamed as she lowered her hands, clearly relieved to see that no one had a gun pointed at her. Her voice gained confidence as she continued. "I saw you come out here and I wanted to check on you, make sure you were alright. But then I heard you talking about Cassandra and I— Like I said, I didn't want to interrupt."

"That's alright," Abby said. "Paxton's getting a golf cart, he'll be back any minute."

A flicker of hesitation passed. Abby wondered if this was actually new information or if Sabrina was calculating how to respond. She prompted, "But I guess you would know that if you followed us here, right?"

"I couldn't hear anything through the storm," Sabrina said. "I just saw you come inside and Paxton leave. I thought maybe there'd been some sort of argu-ment. I wanted to make sure you were okay."

"So you snuck in the back door and hid like some kind of stalker?" Elena's fists clenched at her sides, her gaze boring into Sabrina's. "Is that what you did the night Cassandra died too?"

Sabrina's face paled. "What?"

"Cassandra followed someone into the woods that night," Abby explained, realizing they had narrowed it down to either Nick or Sabrina. It felt pretty suspicious that Sabrina had followed them out here if she was innocent. "Was it you?"

The silence stretched for a moment. Abby expected Sabrina to deny it or burst into tears and give some harmless explanation—anything to prove her innocence. But her eyes narrowed as she folded her arms across her chest, her foot tapping restlessly against the floor. "Who told you that?"

"Cassandra," Abby said.

Sabrina blinked, the flashlight's golden rays falling over her narrow shoulders, making her look larger and tougher than usual. "When did she tell you this?"

"A few days ago."

"She's alive?" Relief swept over Sabrina so powerfully, it washed away her mask. She practically trembled as she glanced over her shoulder, as if expecting Cassandra to make an appearance at any moment.

"She's dead," Abby clarified. "We spoke with her ghost."

Sabrina stared at Abby, before she broke into a nervous laugh. It was cut short when she realized no one was joining in. She gulped. "You're serious?"

"Where were you going the night she died?" Elena pressed.

"Nowhere." Sabrina's voice pitched higher—with fear or annoyance, Abby couldn't be sure. "I was in my cabin, asleep, same as everyone else."

"Except whoever Cassandra followed," Elena pointed out.

"I liked Cassandra. Why would I kill her? Why would I sneak out in the middle of the night?" She paused and then added, "Except to follow you two—to make sure you didn't get hurt."

"How did you follow us?" Abby asked. Sabrina's cabin was on the other side of the shared bathroom, and Abby had been careful not to shine her flashlight in that direction.

"I told you, I saw you sneak out. I figured something really important—and possibly dangerous—must be going on if you were both sneaking out in a storm together, leaving the kids alone."

The word *together* struck Abby as suspicious. If Sabrina had really been watching them, wouldn't she have known that Elena snuck out first, then Abby and Lilly. Sabrina hadn't mentioned Lilly, which made Abby wonder if she was lying. And if she was lying, why?

"You saw us leaving together?" Abby asked, trying to keep her tone casual enough to keep Sabrina from being suspicious. "And you followed us the whole way here without checking on our cabin?"

"I didn't want to lose track of you."

"Abby and I didn't leave together," Elena said, eyes narrowing.

Sabrina shifted her weight. "You both left. I didn't think the details were important."

"Who left first?" Elena asked, crossing her arms.

"I don't know, it was dark. All I saw was someone adult-sized leaving and then another adult-sized person followed. I assumed you'd spaced it out to look less suspicious."

"You didn't see any kids?"

Sabrina hesitated, then shook her head. "It was dark. If anyone else was with you, I wouldn't have noticed. I didn't even realize Paxton was with you until you got here."

"You didn't see anything with Cassandra, then?" Abby asked. "Didn't see Elena twist her ankle?"

"I was keeping my distance."

"What time did we leave?" Abby asked.

Sabrina folded her arms across her chest, her bright pink nail polish striking against her pale skin. "What's with the third-degree questions? Clearly, I'm here. I followed you. Can we just…wait here in peace until Paxton gets back with that golf cart?"

"I don't think you followed us," Abby said.

"Why else would I be here?"

"I think you did come for us." Abby tried to make sense of her thoughts. For some reason, she couldn't draw her gaze away from where Sabrina tapped her fingernails against her arm. "But I don't think you saw us sneak out. Somehow, you knew we were here, but you didn't follow us."

Her *pink* fingernails—they were the same shade of pink as the blanket she had found with the kittens. Sabrina had been here before. She'd found those kittens, cared for them. Abby pointed at the camera's blinking red light. "You saw us on that."

"Okay, fine," Sabrina said. "Yes, I put the camera up. But is that a crime?"

"Why do you have a camera in the middle of an abandoned building in the woods?" Elena demanded.

"There's a cat colony," Sabrina said. "I take care of them."

Abby felt a wave of frustration that it had taken her

so long to put the pieces together, which was soon followed by guilt at how harshly she had pressured Sabrina. Everything she said made sense. Of course she wasn't hiding a confession of murder, just a slightly rebellious act of charity. She sighed, leaving behind a sense of disappointment. She had felt so close to solving this case, to finding out who really killed Cassandra, but she had been chasing the wrong clues and made a bad impression on Lucas's new girlfriend.

"We rescued the kittens," Abby said, hoping to get back on her good side. "In case you were wondering."

"I saw," Sabrina replied with a sigh. "Through the camera feed. Also, the girls keep faking sick so they can see the kittens. So, I assumed they ended up with that nurse girlfriend of yours."

The air seemed to grow colder and Abby shivered, rubbing her damp jeans for warmth.

Elena shook her head, as if she didn't believe Sabrina. "Is that what you were doing the night Cass died? Sneaking out to feed the cats?"

"Of course not."

The doorknob rattled. It twisted and the door creaked open.

Mina stood in the rain.

"It's so good to see you," Abby called in relief, pulling Mina into a hug. Mina remained stiff, her zip-up hoodie slipping off her shoulder, skin cold to the touch. Abby stepped back in alarm, expecting to find her shivering, but she remained steady, stoic. Her eyes were…wrong. They appeared to be filled with a pale gray mist. A ghostly mist.

Abby took a cautious step back, chills running down her spine as Lucas's fears about possession played in her mind.

"I need to speak with Elena," she said in a curt, un-Mina-like tone.

"Cassandra?" Abby asked, taking another step back.

Elena flinched away from her. Abby couldn't blame her. The sight of Mina with her vacant misty eyes was unsettling, even if she was possessed by a mostly friendly ghost. "I want to help you. I promise, Cass! I want to find who did this to you."

Abby raced to her briefcase, flipping through loose notes and pamphlets she had skimmed, trying to recall the cure to possession. There had to be a way to get Mina back. She wished desperately that Lucas was here. He would know what to do. She glanced back at Mina, trying her best to remain calm and appear as if she were in control of the situation—was Mina in there? Could she somehow get through to her?

Sabrina was clapping. "I'm sorry, but if this little theatrical production is some weird way to get me to confess to a murder I didn't commit, it's not going to work. A+ for effort though."

Mina-Cassandra turned to Sabrina and Sabrina stepped toward her, clearly thinking this was an act. "Nice contacts."

"Sabrina?" Mina—no, Cassandra—asked, tilting her head unnaturally in Sabrina's direction.

Abby winced. It was extremely unsettling to hear a ghost use her girlfriend's voice, not to mention what she was doing with her body. She picked up the salt gun and tucked it into the back of her pajama pants, just in case things got out of hand. She didn't want to do anything that could potentially hurt Mina.

God, how had she let Mina get possessed? Cassandra had seemed like such a calm, innocent ghost —and she was turning out to be the most dangerous one yet. She doubted she *wanted* to hurt Mina, but if she wasn't careful, she would. The thought of Mina being lost forever to some ghostly presence shook her to her core. Her knees wobbled. There had to be a way to free her. They needed to send Cassandra on—whether they figured out who killed her or not.

Sabrina patted Mina's arm and her eyes widened. "God, you're freezing! Do you have dry ice or something in your pockets?"

"Elena, do you have anything of Cassandra's that was meaningful to her? A necklace or a diary or… something she kept with her all the time?"

Elena wasn't listening. She stood, took a tentative, painful-looking step toward Cassandra. "I don't know who you followed that night, but it wasn't me!" She pointed a trembling finger at Sabrina. "Could it have been her?"

Sabrina folded her arms around her chest, clearly annoyed, but waited patiently in silence as Cassandra circled her. She moved slower, dragging each step, as if she wasn't quite used to walking.

"Like I said before," Sabrina said with a huff, "I didn't go anywhere. I was in my cabin, asleep. Not running around in the woods."

Abby turned her attention to Sabrina. "How did you know Cassandra died in the woods? The news said she went out in a canoe, right? But you just mentioned the woods."

"Well, that's where we are now, isn't it?" Sabrina sighed in exasperation. "I just meant I wasn't outside, anywhere."

Maybe they were getting somewhere with Sabrina. Maybe she had been there the night Cassandra died. She definitely seemed to be hiding something. But Mina was in trouble and they didn't have time to keep gathering clues and forming theories.

"Sabrina," Cassandra said gently. She brushed a strand of damp hair from Sabrina's face and stared at her fingers, as if surprised by her own actions. "You used to wear butterfly clips."

Sabrina leaned away from her, glaring. "If you expect me to believe you're Cassandra, you'll have to do better than that."

"On my first day as a counselor, you told me not to worry if I mess up, because the kids will only know something is wrong if I act like something is wrong."

Sabrina's eyes widened. "How do you know that? How are you doing this?"

"Because it's me," Cassandra snapped. She shoved an index finger against Sabrina's chest. "And I remember you dropped a butterfly clip that night. It really *was* you. The last person I saw before I died."

Sabrina flinched and inched toward the door.

Well, that certainly made her look guilty. Of all the counselors, why did it have to be the one that Lucas was dating? She had seemed too kind and thoughtful for murder. But as panic and fear flickered across her features, the pieces began to fall into place.

Abby moved to block her path, but Cassandra was faster. Cassandra grabbed her wrist, holding her back. "You had a box. You were burying something."

"What were you burying, Sabrina?" Elena asked.

Sabrina tried to slip free as she glanced between the two of them.

The front door opened, spilling rain into the room. Paxton ran in, followed by Lucas and Nick.

Paxton halted as he took in the situation. "Someone should have told me this was a party. I'd have brought pizza."

"Uh, what's wrong with Mina?" Lucas asked, slinking to Abby's side. "Please don't tell me she's possessed."

"She's possessed," Abby confirmed, trying not to let the full depth of her fear show.

Lucas made a sound like a tea kettle about to boil. "I *knew* it. I knew someone was going to get possessed sooner or later."

"Do you know how to get her unpossessed?" Desperation seeped through Abby's voice.

Sabrina attempted to shove Cassandra away, but Cassandra—or Mina—was too strong. She yanked Sabrina's arm and Sabrina cried out in pain.

Abby's chest constricted. "Don't hurt her!" she shouted at the same time as Lucas. They glanced at one another.

"It was Sabrina," Abby said in a rush, trying to

warn him. "She's the one Cassandra followed that night!"

Nick moved toward Cassandra. "Is there a problem here?"

"No!" Elena cried, removing the binoculars from around her neck. She thrust them toward Nick. "It's Cass! She's communicating with us."

Nick's jaw clenched, eyebrows pinching together. He glanced from Sabrina to Elena, and then at Mina's haunted eyes. "This can't be true. Can it?"

"It can't be," Lucas agreed, taking the binoculars from Elena and setting them on the windowsill. "If Sabrina went out that night, I'm sure there's a perfectly reasonable explanation for it, right, Sabrina?"

Sabrina's lower lip trembled as she struggled against Cassandra's grip.

"Lucas," Abby hissed. The rest of the room was silent. "Any ideas about how to get Mina back?"

Lucas ran his hands over his coiled hair. He looked torn between answering Abby and rushing to Sabrina's side. He said, "We can either help the spirit move on, or we need to help Mina break its hold."

"How do we do that?"

"Something important to her—to Mina. Something sentimental or someone she loves—" He tore his gaze from Sabrina to face Abby. "You could try to get through to her."

Abby's fear rose. While it was clear Mina had feelings for her, she wasn't sure they were deep enough to be considered love. She wasn't even sure if her own feelings could be considered love, let alone if they were reciprocated. She loosened the cord of the salt pendant around her neck. "What about salt?"

"Salt can weaken it, but once someone's possessed, you'd need a lot more salt than we have to break their hold."

Abby tried not to panic. She was the one who had dragged Mina into this whole ghost business. If Mina got hurt—

Abby wouldn't let that happen. She would do anything to keep Mina safe. "We have to send Cassandra on."

"I don't think we can do that without solving her murder."

"Fine," Abby rounded on Sabrina. "What were you doing in the woods?"

Lucas gave Abby a look of betrayal.

"Okay, yes, I was there." Sabrina's eyes flashed between Abby and a very intimidating Cassandra. "But I didn't see what happened to you. I'm sorry."

Sabrina twisted out of Cassandra's grip, throwing herself to the floor. She scrambled to her feet and raced to the door, rattling the knob. Someone had shut the latch. She tried to unlock it, but the latch stuck.

"Let me go!" She screamed, turning to face everyone as Cassandra moved toward her, dragging each step.

"You must have some idea what happened," Cassandra said casually, as if remarking that it was, in fact, raining. "You must have seen the killer, even if you didn't recognize them."

Abby stared at Sabrina, her face lit by several flashlights and the faint red blinking of the camera. Everything was leading back to Sabrina being the killer, but Abby couldn't figure out *why*.

"What were you burying, Sabrina?" Elena demanded. "Did you kill someone else too that night? And then you killed Cassandra because she saw you burying the body?"

Sabrina pressed her back against the door as Cassandra advanced. "No! No, I wasn't even the last one who saw her—ask Nick!"

Stunned silence filled the room. Elena alone made a sound of rage or frustration as all eyes—and flashlight beams—turned to Nick.

"What the hell are you talking about?"

"I saw you," Sabrina continued. "When I was on my way back to the cabins—you were out in a canoe. The same canoe they said Cassandra ran off in."

Cassandra tilted her head to the side. "I never got in a canoe."

"Right," Sabrina said. "But he was there! And he was so upset you dumped him. He could have rowed to shore and killed you."

"I knew it!" Elena shouted, storming toward Nick. "I knew it was you!"

Paxton stepped between them, holding out his arms in an attempt to keep the peace. He asked in a strangled voice, "Is this true?"

"Of course not," Nick said. "I took the canoe out that night to dump some alcohol bottles—you remember how they were going to search our rooms? Well, I figured it wasn't worth the trouble. And you saw what happened when they found a beer can in the trash —the whole place freaked out. Imagine if they'd found three bottles of vodka."

"I saw you that night," Cassandra said slowly. "I didn't know it was you, but just before I went into the woods, I watched you get out of the canoe. It drifted off and you waded out after it."

"It was dark. The rope slipped," Nick admitted. "I wasn't able to reach it."

"That's the canoe they found," Abby realized. "All this time, the news thought it was Cassandra's, but it was yours. Why didn't you say anything?"

"I thought she ran away," Nick said. "I figured it would help us both out if they thought it was hers—I wouldn't have to explain what I was doing out on a lake in the middle of the night and she could get a clean getaway."

"But it's been years," Elena protested. "You could have at least told me."

"And have you use it against me? We both know you would have gone straight to the police. But now that Cass is here, she can testify I didn't kill her!" Nick fist-pumped the air and quickly straightened up, seem- ingly remembering that this wasn't a celebratory occasion.

"You're still a thief," Lucas muttered.

"What was that?"

"I said you're still a thief," Lucas said, louder but less confident. "Selling things you find on the beach."

"Selling what now?" Nick asked, sounding

genuinely surprised. "Things I found on the beach? You mean that Rolex?"

"What Rolex?" Paxton asked.

Nick shook his head. "One time, years ago, we found a Rolex washed up on shore. I thought—how could someone just leave money like that lying around? I had this idea to get it fixed up and sold, and use the money for Johnny. But I never did. One day, it was gone. I assumed the original owner had come back for it. The only person I told any of this to was you, Sabrina."

All eyes turned back to Sabrina, who was still hiding what she had been doing out in the woods— which meant it was probably not good. Definitely against camp rules.

Sabrina met Nick's gaze. She shook her head as if silently pleading with him to take the words back.

"Sabrina," Abby said softly. "What were you doing in the woods that night?"

"It's not important." Sabrina's composure was slipping, her words trembling.

"She's scared," Lucas said, jumping to her defense. "We've had a long night. Why don't we all go back to our cabins and talk through this in the morning?"

"Whatever it was, you wanted to keep it a secret, didn't you?" Abby ventured, keeping her eyes locked on Sabrina. "Cassandra wasn't supposed to be there. She wasn't supposed to see."

Sabrina shook her head—whether she was denying Abby's accusations or pleading for her to stop, Abby couldn't be sure. She continued forming her theory aloud. "You want to know what I think? I think you liked Nick's plan. I think *you* took the Rolex and sold it. Didn't you?"

Sabrina whimpered.

Lucas started to move to Sabrina's side, but Abby held out a hand in warning. She wasn't finished. "And it didn't stop there. That box in the boat shed that you claimed was Nick's had some nice jewelry. I'm not sure how much, exactly, it would go for, but I bet it would be enough to buy some nice designer clothes."

"Sabrina, you didn't," Lucas said in shock.

"I'm pretty sure she did," Abby said. "Because—while I'm not the biggest jewelry person—you know what I noticed? A pearl necklace. I remember seeing it and thinking how my late girlfriend had one just like it. And, Sabrina, weren't you wearing a pearl necklace at Jason and Hannah's engagement party?"

"You were," Lucas said, his face falling. "Oh god, Sabrina, what did you do?"

Sabrina looked like she was struggling to respond.

Cassandra closed in on Sabrina in an instant—moving so close, the drawstrings of Mina's hoodie battered her nose. "Yeah, Sabrina, what did you *do?*"

"It was an accident," Sabrina whispered, her whole body trembling.

Her words hung in the air. Abby sucked in a breath. Was this a confession?

"What was an accident?" Nick demanded.

Sabrina sobbed, her eyes glistening as she turned to Nick. At last, she got out a single word: "Cassandra."

All the pieces came together—Sabrina, having

traded in the Rolex for cash, burying the cash or other stolen goods in the woods, afraid that the police would find them in their search for alcohol. Cassandra, following her, thinking she was Elena. Considering they were a similar height and build, it would be an easy mistake to make in the dark.

In the silence that followed, Abby could sense everyone else coming to the same conclusion. She'd thought there would be a sense of relief at the closure, but there was only greater pain—pain that someone so many of these people had considered a friend had done something so awful. And pain at the reminder that Cassandra was gone, and Sabrina's confession wouldn't bring her back. Even the wind sounded like it was mourning.

Nick locked his fingers behind his head and leaned forward like he was going to be sick. "Shit."

Lucas made a strangled sound like a whimper. Abby put a hand on his shoulder and rubbed soothing circles on his back. He would get through this.

"I—I thought she was the police," Sabrina stammered, inching away from Cassandra, whose head was bowed, her face somber and thoughtful.

"Why?" Paxton asked softly, eyes sparkling with tears.

"Because they were out here looking for people! You remember the party. I didn't want to go to jail."

"So you killed someone?" Elena asked, her voice rising. "You killed Cass over a goddamn Rolex?"

Sabrina chewed her lip. "Not just a watch."

Nick brought a fist to his lips. "Jesus!"

"What the hell, Sabrina?" Paxton began to pace. "If you needed money, you could have just asked to borrow some."

Elena laughed bitterly. "Where's the fun in that, right? You're a murderer and a thief. I bet she was stealing from you too, Paxton. Weren't you, Sabrina?"

"No," Sabrina insisted. "I didn't steal from anyone, I swear. Everything I sold was just stuff I found."

"Found where?" Elena demanded. "In the Lodge? In people's pockets?"

"Here!" Sabrina waved her hands at the empty room.

Elena scoffed. The house seemed to groan in protest as it settled. Paxton's flashlight darted over the peeling paint and bare walls, with nails and hooks where picture frames had once been. "What is this place? How come it's not on any maps?"

"I've been here before." Nick rubbed his eyes as if that would help him better recall. "Years ago. This is where we hid that summer—just a few weeks before Cassandra died. I remember thinking how odd it was to find an abandoned house in the woods. It was different then. Less…empty. There were portraits, and mirrors, and furniture—"

Something about his words sent a surge of excitement through Abby. She couldn't believe she hadn't thought of it before. She exchanged a glance with Lucas. Was he thinking what she was thinking?

Lucas shook his head. "Don't say it."

Elena frowned. "Don't say what?"

"This could be the legendary lost house." Abby had to say it. "The one that belonged to Sobbing Molly."

A heavy silence followed, broken by the pounding of rain and rustle of windswept branches.

Sabrina scoffed. "That's a children's story. Look around, there's nothing in this place. Sobbing Molly isn't real."

"She is." Cassandra tilted her head, her misty eyes pointed at a fogged window beside the door. Abby felt chills down her spine as the fog transformed into frost, the faintest shadow appearing in front of it.

She nudged Lucas, who reached for the binoculars. His mouth fell open as he glanced at the window. He promptly lowered them. "Nope. Not tonight. It's too dark and spooky for this, Abby."

Abby took the binoculars from his outstretched palm, too agitated to form a witty response. With a shaky breath, she glanced at Mina, unsure what a possession would look like through the ghostly lenses. She feared that Mina—the real Mina—would be there screaming for help or something. But there was just Cassandra, as clear as if she were living, with only a faint translucent outline of Mina, like some bizarre video filter. It was unnerving, but not as terrifying as Abby had expected.

Abby moved her gaze to the window, where another ghost appeared: a young girl, in a vintage blue and white dress, with dark brown hair pulled back in a half ponytail and tear-filled eyes.

Sobbing Molly. Abby had imagined meeting her a dozen times since she had arrived at Camp Pine

Whispers, but never once had she imagined her showing up in the middle of solving a murder. She asked, in awe and disbelief, "Molly?"

The ghost nodded slowly. She floated toward Sabrina until she was face to face with her. Sabrina shivered.

"This is my home." Molly's voice crackled through the walkie-talkie, clear and firm despite its youthfulness. "You took everything away. My toys, my dresses, my jewelry."

Sabrina trembled as she unclasped the pearl necklace from her neck and tossed it to the floor, raising her hands in surrender. The necklace skidded across the wooden floor, falling still near the front door.

"*Jesus*, Sabrina!" Nick spun around, scanning the walls. "Did you do this? Clear this place out?"

"It was *your* idea!" Sabrina shouted. "You said if someone loses something, it's not stealing."

"I was talking about a watch, not a house," Nick countered. "And I was drunk and eighteen."

"Give them *back*," Molly insisted, the room growing colder with each word.

Sabrina dropped to her knees, cowering. "I *can't*. I sold them, okay? I'm sorry. Please don't hurt me."

"What the hell, Sabrina?" Elena glared up at her, fists clenched. "You killed Cassandra and you robbed this place?"

"It was abandoned!" Sabrina cried. "I needed cash."

She glanced from one person to the next, pleading for them to understand. "My dad's car, remember—he was so upset. He swore he'd make my life miserable until I paid him back for all the damage. That night we hid from the cops here, I took a jewelry box. Just to see if it was worth anything. I thought maybe I could get a hundred bucks or so, but it turns out it was worth *thousands*."

"But all the furniture…" Nick walked deeper into the house, peering past the ladder, into nearly vacant rooms, where there was nothing but a faded rocking chair creaking beside a broken window. "You couldn't have taken it all that summer. You must have been coming back here for years. And you couldn't carry all that. I swear there was a wardrobe, or something like it."

Abby's eyes went to the toolbox. "You didn't carry them, did you? You took them apart."

Sabrina bowed her head, eyes downcast as she seemed to retreat into a shell of herself.

Paxton ran a hand through his damp hair. "I don't understand how no one noticed."

"Every summer, I just took a few pieces," Sabrina explained. "I'd sneak them in my backpack or in a canoe, and store them in the boat shed until I had enough to sell for that year. On the last night of camp, after the kids went home, I'd sneak out at night and carry everything to my trunk."

Nick made a raspy choking sound, a mix of horror and awe. Abby had to agree—Sabrina's plan was clever.

"Just like you, Paxton, and Jason did with my art supplies," Lucas pointed out, shaking his head at Nick.

"Taking one at a time. You thought I wouldn't notice. But I did."

Nick shrugged apologetically, his hands in his pockets, before turning his attention back to Sabrina. His posture immediately shrank; he was clearly distressed by the reminder that she had just confessed to a crime.

"Is that why you killed Cassandra?" Elena demanded. "Because she was onto you?"

"No," Sabrina pleaded. "Like I said, it was an accident. The police were going to search our dorms—and the woods—I couldn't risk them finding bags of cash or antique jewelry under my bunk. It was only a matter of time before they found this place, and it would be cleared out or sold to a museum—so I took as much as I could and buried it."

The words spilled out faster now, as if Sabrina was compelled to get them off her chest. "Cassandra snuck up on me. I thought she was the police. I panicked. I hid until she passed and then I tried to run away, but she was turning toward me and— I just sort of hit her. I didn't mean to. I wasn't thinking. It was dark and I had the shovel and all I could think was that I couldn't get caught. I couldn't go to jail! So I hit her and she fell and hit her head and— I tried to help her, really, I did. But she was, she was—" Sabrina broke into a fit of sobs, her chest heaving as tears streamed down her face. "I didn't know what to do. I ran back to camp and spent the whole night in the bathroom throwing up and crying and— oh, I'm so sorry!"

Abby's stomach knotted with disgust and a twinge of sympathy. Abby felt for the young, scared Sabrina hiding from the police. But killing Cassandra and covering it up, letting her loved ones worry about her for a decade, was cruel, even if the actual murder had been unintentional.

Abby turned to face Cassandra. She couldn't help but wince at the *wrongness* of Mina's face. Not only were her eyes misty, her cheeks were wrinkled into an expression of bitter sorrow. Abby gulped. It was time to get Mina back.

"You have your answer, Cassandra," she said, trying to keep the fear from her voice. "It's time to move on."

A tense wind rose in the center of the room, scattering debris around Sabrina's feet. Abby and Lucas exchanged glances as Abby slowly removed the salt gun from her waistband.

Cassandra lifted a finger to Sabrina, pointing it directly at her heart. "*You* killed me. I don't care what happens next except this: you leave my friends alone. Elena, Nick, Paxton—you don't deserve them. That goes for everyone here at Camp Pine Whispers."

Sabrina nodded, her face tear-stained. "I promise. Oh, Cass, I'm so sorry."

"You better be," Cassandra said, her gaze hardening. "You better be sorry every day of your life. But know that I will *never* forgive you."

Abby aimed the salt gun, but kept her finger off the trigger as Cassandra shut her eyes, a softness overcoming her expression.

And just like that, Cassandra's form began to dissipate, her ghostly presence melting under Mina's form until they were two separate entities. Mina staggered and blinked, rubbing her eyes as if she had just woken up.

Abby dropped the salt gun and binoculars and ran to Mina's side, wrapping her arms around her waist. It was such a relief to see her back—alive and well—with warmth running through her cheeks and her warm brown eyes staring back at her.

"Where are we?" Mina asked, glancing around in confusion.

"The house in the woods, where I found Nibbles," Abby explained gently. "How are you feeling?"

"Foggy. But okay." She put a hand on the back of her head and winced. "Was I drugged?"

"Possessed," Lucas clarified.

Mina's face contorted into a look of disgust as Abby rubbed soothing circles along her back. She shot Lucas an annoyed look, hoping to have broken the news with a bit more tact.

"But in good news, Sabrina confessed," Abby added, trying to sound cheerful.

Mina's eyes widened. "To killing Cassandra?"

Elena let out a choked sob. Paxton moved behind her, placing a comforting hand on her shoulder, his own eyes glistening with tears.

Nick whistled. "What the hell, Sabrina? All this time, you haven't said a word!"

"I didn't want to go to jail."

"Well, you're going," Elena snapped.

The fallen necklace rose into the air, spinning as it retreated upstairs.

"Is that Molly?" Paxton asked.

"Who?" Mina squinted into the dark.

"Another ghost," Abby said. "I'll explain later. Do they teach you about post-possession care in nursing school?"

"If they do, I missed that chapter."

"It's Molly," Elena said with conviction. "She clearly wants her things back. I don't know we're going to track them all down."

"I'll talk to her," Abby volunteered. "See if there's anything particularly important that can help her move on."

Lucas shifted his weight and whispered gently, "Maybe we should focus on one ghost at a time?"

"Maybe if you had been a better partner, we wouldn't have been dealing with two ghosts at once," Abby said. She instantly regretted it. "Sorry. I didn't mean that. It's just that Mina was possessed and you weren't here and—"

"I get it," Lucas said.

But Abby wasn't finished. "—you're going to Massachusetts and I just… I can't do this without you!"

Abby stared at Lucas, her chest heaving as if she had just scaled the side of a cliff. All her pent-up fears from recent months came crashing down at once.

"Yes, you can," Lucas encouraged.

Abby opened her mouth to deny it and Lucas continued, "But you don't have to. I want to join."

Abby stared at him, stunned. Rain continued to batter the windows, Sabrina's fearful sobs filling the room, but all Abby could focus on was Lucas, in his soaking wet T-shirt and foggy glasses. "What are you saying?"

"I'm saying I want to join Spector Investigations," he said. "Officially. If you'll have me."

Was she dreaming? The words made her heart soar, but she couldn't quite make sense of them. "But what about Massachusetts?"

"I hear they have a lot of ghosts. And I could use a roommate."

Grinning, Abby threw her arms around him, pulling him into a hug. A wild laughter burst from her chest, carrying with it all the fears and worries she had had of them drifting apart. She had never considered the fact that he would want her to move with him. "That would be amazing!"

"Uh, can we maybe save the business planning for when we aren't surrounded by hostile ghosts?" Mina said, pointing to Abby's walkie-talkie.

"Elena." Cassandra's voice crackled through. It sounded weaker, quieter, as if coming from further away.

"Cass?" Elena glanced around hopefully, and Lucas placed the binoculars in her hands.

"I'm sorry, Elena," Cassandra replied. Abby cranked up the volume so she could be heard over the storm. "I should have known you weren't there that night. You were the best sister I could have asked for."

Elena choked back a sob, a sad smile tugging at the corner of her lips.

"Thank you," Cassandra whispered, as a bright light appeared beside Elena. It shimmered and waved, transforming into a faint Cassandra-shaped mist. "All three of you, for making my last summer so wonderful."

Cassandra's otherworldly light filled the room before it dissipated, leaving behind a subtle chill.

Elena lowered the binoculars to wipe trails of mascara-tears from her cheek.

"Is that it?" Nick asked, looking around like he had just woken up at the end of a sport's game and was too sheepish to ask the score. "Is she gone?"

Mina's comforting scent enveloped Abby as she intertwined their fingers and squeezed her palm. "She's at rest."

"Speaking of rest—" Nick yawned. "If we head back now, maybe we'll get some shut eye before the campers wake."

"I'll brew coffee for everyone too wired to sleep," Paxton volunteered. "After I call the police."

Sabrina grimaced at his words, but nodded slowly, accepting there was no more prolonging her fate.

Nick unlocked the door. The lock slid back into place. "What the hell?"

The walkie-talkie crackled again. A younger, softer voice came through. "Please don't leave."

Abby stiffened. "Is that you, Molly?"

"I've been so lonely. Won't you stay?"

"We need to get back," Abby said carefully. "If we promise to come back tomorrow, will you let us leave?"

As the walkie-talkie continued to spill static through the room, the deadbolt unlocked and the door creaked open.

"That's creepy as shit," Nick said, opening the door wider and inspecting the deadbolt.

"Thank you, Molly," Elena said, leaning against Paxton as she hobbled forward. "I'll be back tomorrow."

Abby was impressed by how well she had picked up interacting with ghosts—even if she didn't know how to use the equipment. She considered coming back to show her another time. Maybe she could help them find a way to help Sobbing Molly move on. But that was a task for another day.

Tonight, all they had to do was make it back to camp.

Chapter Twenty-Three

The mountains turned blue before the sun rose, mist parting as birds began to chirp. The skies had cleared somewhen in the night and Abby cradled herself in a blanket as she leaned back in a rocking chair, her borrowed slippers brushing the dewy wooden slats worn from years of use.

It had been a long night. Too long. Even though Abby had tried to fall asleep—once Sabrina was safely in police custody and Elena had retreated back to the cabin—her mind raced too much. She kept replaying the night's events: Sobbing Molly's surprise appearance, Sabrina's tearful confession, and—worst of all—Mina's possessed, misty eyes. Abby shuddered. She should never have gotten her involved with ghosts. If she hadn't come here looking for Sobbing Molly, they wouldn't have run into Cassandra, and Mina would be tucked safely in a trailer somewhere—or better yet, at home with Abby after a normal date, like dinner and a movie.

Abby felt a pang of longing to be able to take Mina to a movie without having a panic attack or a flashback to the night Chelsea died.

A door slid open behind her and Mina's familiar scent put her at ease as she slid into the chair beside Abby.

"I brought you coffee," Mina offered, holding out a mug. "With sugar. So much sugar."

"You know just how I like it." Abby took the mug with a grin, savoring the warmth against her palms. Steam rose in a curl, tickling her knuckles. It tasted delicious.

"I figured." Mina smiled, though it was somewhat forced, like she wanted to say more, but wasn't sure how. She tapped her nails against her mug. Without her usual rings, her fingers looked naked and fragile. Her usual air of confidence was diminished by the slouch in her shoulders, the way she chewed her lower lip, and her downcast eyes.

Even if she had managed to fall asleep, the night had been hard on her—what with the possession and all. Abby wanted to ask what it felt like, but she wasn't sure how.

Wind hummed through the trees, rustling leaves and flowers as the sky brightened with the first rays of dawn.

"I'm sorry," Abby said quickly.

Mina glanced at her curiously. "For what?"

"For roping you into this—" She gestured between them.

"I don't think you roped me into anything. From what I recall, *I* seduced *you*." She wiggled her eyebrows.

Abby couldn't help but laugh, feeling the tension dissipate from her shoulders. "The seduction was mutual. But the ghost thing? You never signed up for that."

"Actually, I did." Mina inched toward her. "I knew about that when we started dating. It's one of the things that drew me to you—the fact that you pursued something with such passion. And not only do you enjoy it, you help them—spirits that are trapped or stuck—you help them from the goodness of your heart. Do you know how rare it is to find someone who would take the time to help—not one, but multiple—ghosts move on?"

Abby felt her heart warm at the words. "But it's dangerous."

"So is stunt work. What's a little danger, if you love what you do?"

"You got *possessed*."

"For like half an hour, tops." Mina took a sip of her coffee. "I can't say I enjoyed it, but I've been through worse. I'm just glad she didn't make me do ballet. My legs aren't built for pirouettes."

Abby studied her for signs that she was masking her true feelings. Finding none, she ventured, "So, you're not upset?"

"Of course not."

Abby felt herself slouching forward in relief as Mina continued. "The girl was murdered. We helped catch her murderer. I think that's worth a bit of time lost, don't you?"

Before Abby could answer, the door squeaked open and Lucas stuck his head out. "Sorry to interrupt. Paxton got donuts. I thought you might want some."

He held up a plate with two steaming glazed donuts.

"You thought right, thanks!" Abby reached for the nearest one. It was warm and soft in her hand and practically melted on her tongue.

Mina took the other a bit more gracefully and gestured to an empty chair beside her. "You're welcome to join us."

"Thanks, but I'm almost finished getting our new website set up. Check it out." He opened the door wider and retreated inside, returning moments later with his laptop. He held the screen that read *Spector and Clark Paranormal Investigations* toward Mina.

Mina scanned the text, a smile creeping over her features. "I love it! Especially the contact section. 'Who you gonna—"

Lucas gasped, turning to Abby with a grin. "You showed her *Ghostbusters*!"

"Only the new one," Abby admitted.

Lucas clicked his tongue. "Shame."

Mina's laughter lifted Abby's spirits as Lucas closed his laptop and tucked it under his arm, shaking his head.

"I'm sorry it turned out to be Sabrina," Abby said. Lucas's face fell and she felt a fresh wave of sympathy toward him.

Lucas shrugged, his emotions masked. That meant he had been up all night crying about it and was now over the worst of it, or he was refusing to acknowledge how he felt and the grief would hit him full force in a few hours or days. "Like you said, she bent her books. It was doomed from the start."

Abby grinned, relieved to see he still had his sense of humor.

"You know, what I can't figure out," he said, adjusting his glasses, "is how no one discovered that house until she did."

"And Nick," Abby reminded him.

"Paxton talked to his parents about it," he continued. "They had no clue it was there. He wants to restore it, see if he can't do something to help send Sobbing Molly on. I thought about offering to help, but you know how much I hate manual labor, and there's only a week left of camp so…"

Mina took the last bite of her donut and rubbed her fingers together, sending tiny flakes of dried sugar to the balcony floor. "I mean, it was pretty well hidden. I'm more confused about why the police never found Cassandra's body. A girl goes missing and they just stop looking?"

"The lake is really big," Lucas pointed out. "And there was so much damage from that storm—not to mention another storm a few days later. With so much land, the forest was probably a mess—full of dead trees, mudslides, landslides."

"There was that sign," Abby said, snapping her fingers. "The one about landslides. Do you think that was real, or do you think that was just a rumor started to keep people from finding Sobbing Molly's house?"

"It's real," Lucas said. "Did you see the damage after last night? Not to mention that pile of rocks you kept climbing to get up to that clearing where we first saw Cassandra. I'll bet you anything that was caused by a landslide decades ago."

"Would you bet me your car?"

"No," Lucas admitted. "Twenty bucks."

"Maybe that's how the house stayed hidden." Mina twirled a strand of hair around her index finger. "Those rocks could have hidden that house even better until they fell in a landslide, making it more accessible the summer Sabrina and Nick stumbled across it."

Lucas's eyes lit up. "We know there was a storm earlier that summer—when Sabrina had her car accident—that could have been what triggered the landslide."

At least he could say her name without wincing. That was progress.

"After that, Sabrina probably worked hard to keep it hidden," Mina pointed out.

"I like to think Sobbing Molly kept it hidden," said Abby. "Maybe she brought those kittens there to lure us in, to figure out what Sabrina was up to."

"That's a theory," Lucas said skeptically, retreating back inside.

Mina shrugged. "With ghosts, anything's possible."

Abby leaned back, taking in a deep breath of fresh morning air as she watched the sun's golden rays fall across the campgrounds.

This may not be the life she envisioned for herself, but she was happy here, with her friends—with Mina, whose mere presence grounded her and whose smile made her heart flutter. This was what made working with ghosts worth it in the end—the simple fact that life goes on, and people heal, and love grows in wide and unexpected directions.

Her heart went out to the ghosts that didn't have that chance.

Abby twisted her salt necklace and made a promise to herself: she wouldn't let her past hold her back from living. Not anymore.

"Abby?" Mina was standing in the doorway, one hand on the door frame, her favorite flannel shirt draped over her tank top. Dark hair swayed gently around her face, her expression soft. She looked peaceful, at ease. Abby wanted to wake up every morning and see her like this. "You ready to head in?"

"I love you," Abby blurted out. As soon as the words left her mouth, she knew they were true. She felt the warmth in her heart every time she brushed Mina's fingers or smelled her shampoo or heard her make a sarcastic remark. But she felt it most in the quiet moments—whether they were together or apart, when her heart longed to be nearer to Mina. Or maybe it just longed for Abby to make sure she didn't lose her.

Mina's lips parted, her eyes widening in surprise before her face settled into a smirk. "It's about time."

"It's fine if you don't say it back," Abby said, jumping to her feet. "I just wanted you to—"

Her words were cut off as Mina stepped forward

and wrapped her arms around Abby's shoulders, brushing her lips against Abby's in a warm, passionate kiss. Pulling back, she cupped Abby's chin in her warm fingers and said, "I'm just jealous you beat me to saying it. I had a whole night planned. It involved pizza and those video games you love that I suck at."

"*Pac-Man?* Or *Mario Kart?*"

"Both. I guess there's no point in waiting now, is there?" She sighed, her breath tingling Abby's neck. "I love you, too, Abby."

The words settled into Abby's heart like a final puzzle piece, making her feel whole and safe and *alive.* Her heart beat with a triumphant cheer.

"If I recall correctly," Mina whispered, her sensual voice sending pleasant shivers down Abby's spine, "I believe you owe me a favor."

"I do," Abby agreed as Mina pressed a warm kiss into her neck. "So many favors."

"Time to pay up." Mina wrapped her strong arms around Abby's waist and pulled her in close.

As the sky turned pink and sunlight flooded the balcony, Abby had better things to think about than ghosts.

Acknowledgements

Wow, here we are at book three! When I first dreamed up Abby and her ghostly adventures, I wasn't sure how far we'd get since a 'queer ghost mystery with psych vibes' was very niche. I was happy to see it transform into what it has—a warm, heartfelt story about moving on and falling in love. And I couldn't have done it without so many supportive readers who provided enthusiasm and encouragement along the way.

This book wouldn't exist if it wasn't for my love of ghost stories, which I attribute to the fantastic 'spooky' bedtime stories my Grandpa told me as a child—Grandpa, I bet you never imagined I'd still be telling (and asking for) ghost stories in my thirties!

This book also wouldn't be the same if it wasn't for my love of North Carolina's Blue Ridge Mountains, which were unfortunately severely damaged by Hurricane Helene in 2024. As I'm writing this, many parts of the mountains are still recovering. My heart goes out to everyone who was impacted by the storm, and I'm grateful for everyone who has helped rebuild places so dear to me.

A special thank you must go out to my beta readers —Farren Benvenuti, Mason Burgess, Stevie Burgess, and Ivy Moe. Your feedback was invaluable and made this story much stronger (and will hopefully save people the trouble of screaming 'where's the f***ing camera' that I apparently forgot to mention).

Thank you to Hannah McCall at Black Cat Editorial Services for providing yet another fantastic line edit. I always appreciate your insights and attention to detail! And to Holly Dunn for providing such gorgeous cover art. Thanks for making my books stand out on the shelves!

And of course, Kiran—thank you for being the best wife I could possibly imagine and for supporting my writing dreams.

About the Author

Morgan Spellman grew up in North Carolina, where he listened to too many ghost stories and stayed up late to sneak episodes of *Buffy the Vampire Slayer*. As a trans man, he writes heartwarming stories inspired by the fantasy adventures and charming cozy mysteries he devoured in early adulthood, with LGBTQ+ characters front and center. When he's not writing, reading, or working his day job, you'll likely find him playing Dungeons & Dragons, reading his wife's fanfiction, or binge-watching mysteries with his cats.

For more books and updates visit: Morganspellman.com